# Tempest's Course

## Other books in the Quilts of Love Series

# TEMPEST'S COURSE

## Quilts of Love Series

Lynette Sowell

*a novel approach to faith*

*Tempest's Course*

ISBN-13: 978-1-4267-5276-6

Published by Abingdon Press, P.O. Box 801, Nashville, TN 37202
www.abingdonpress.com

Published in association with the MacGregor Literary Agency.

Library of Congress Cataloging-in-Publication Data

Sowell, Lynette.
    Tempest's course / Lynette Sowell.
      pages cm. — (Quilts of Love Series)
    ISBN 978-1-4267-5276-6 (binding: adhesive, pbk. : alk. paper)  1.  Quilts—Fiction. 2.
Quilting—Fiction. 3.  Restoration and conservation—Fiction.  I. Title.
    PS3619.O965T46 2013
    813'.6—dc23

                                                                            2013014475

Printed in the United States of America

1 2 3 4 5 6 7 8 9 10 / 18 17 16 15 14 13

*For C.J., who always makes me feel like I've just come home. Thanks for letting me drag you around New Bedford's cobblestone streets in December when it was only thirty degrees outside.*

## Acknowledgments

With many thanks to Camille Breeze and her crew at Museum Textile Services of Andover, Massachusetts. You welcomed me to your studio, let me pick your brain about textile conservation, taught me about the different personalities of conservators, and offered me many resources to help my heroine deal with a 150-year-old quilt. Any omissions or inaccuracies are entirely my own.

I am grateful for the help of the staff at the New Bedford Whaling National Historical Park for answering my questions and letting me peek at the world of a whaling captain's family, as well as the New Bedford that once was.

To the staff of the Rotch-Jones-Duff House on famous County Street in New Bedford, thank you for letting us feel like we had the run of the place when we visited. I felt like I'd truly discovered the inside of Gray House.

Lastly, kudos to Destination Soups of New Bedford for making a "wicked" clam chowder that warmed us up on a very chilly research day.

*God settles the lonely in their homes;*
*he sets prisoners free with happiness,*
*but the rebellious dwell in a parched land.*
—Psalm 68:6

# Prologue

*April 1853*
*New Bedford, Massachusetts*

They say a madwoman cannot make sense of the world around her, let alone write about it, but I can. My empty arms are now full, but my heart tells me that it will never be full again. The one light of my life is gone from me, and I have no embers from which to coax a new spark.

My atonement is futile. I have no other choice than the one before me. If Almighty God is listening from Heaven, surely He will accept this sacrifice. Perhaps the generations to follow will as well.

# 1

*Present Day*

Kelly Frost tried not to shiver as she stood on the sidewalk in front of Gray House, but she did anyway. The breeze drifting from New Bedford's waterfront had some bite in it, even for May. Kelly squinted against the sun's glare reflecting off a car door, now slammed shut.

An efficient-looking woman made her way with precise steps to the gate that protected the front lawn of Gray House from nosy passersby and visitors. "Sorry I'm late. I would have told you to meet me at the real estate office, but the house is closer." She unlocked the gate and swung it open. The iron-work complained at the disturbance.

"Not a problem," Kelly said as she followed the woman—Mrs. Acres, was it?—up the cobbled sidewalk, then the wooden steps.

"I've been instructed to open the house for you while you complete your assessment of the piece, then lock up when you're ready to go." Mrs. Acres now worked the front door lock with an ancient key. "How long do you think you'll need?"

"An hour, most likely." She'd made assessments of antique and ancient textiles before, and this current request should be little different from other times in the past.

"I'll be back in two. Mincie's at the groomers, and she'll be done before you will be." Mrs. Acres leaned on the front door, then bumped it with her shoulder. "Stubborn door. I can't tell you the last time we opened the place up."

The heavy wooden door swung inward, and the scent of closed-up house—stale air and dust—struck them. Something tickled the inside of Kelly's nose, but it was Mrs. Acres who sneezed.

"Oh my, the dust." Mrs. Acres shook her head. "Do you know where the quilt is?"

Kelly nodded. "I was told the quilt should be in the master bedroom on the second floor. The one with the Italian marble fireplace." She hoped the lady wouldn't start a long conversation. Small talk made her itch, like freshly mown grass. She shifted her tote bag on her shoulder.

"Two hours, and I'll be back." Mrs. Acres turned on her heel, then paused before she exited the house. "Don't steal the silver. We count it." With that, she gave a little giggle and shut the front door behind her.

The entryway alone made Kelly stare. What woodwork. The curved banister of the great main staircase snaked upward to the second floor. As she stood in the entryway, she could see down a long hallway with rooms off each side. Immediately to her right stood a set of wooden pocket doors. Her curious bent made her want to start walking, room by room, to see what treasures lay inside. Or dust magnets, rather. Now it was her turn to sneeze.

Instead, thoughts of her skinny bank account spurred her to take the creaking stairs to the second floor and find the master bedroom. Depending on the work required to restore the quilt, she hoped to at least pay the bills for the rest of the year. Beyond that, well, she'd figure something out. She always did, because she'd always had to.

The wood of the banister was cool and smooth under her fingertips. Again, the history hanging in the air made her pause at the top of the steps. The house supposedly hadn't had a resident in at least fifty years, perhaps longer. Or so Mrs. Acres had guessed. Kelly stepped from room to room, to see which one had the marble fireplace. Furniture draped in heavy cloth would probably resemble ghosts at night, with moonbeams streaming through the window glass. Even in the daytime, her overactive imagination caused another shiver, this one not from a cool breeze. Which room? She'd counted no less than four chimneys sprouting from the rooftop when she stood outside. That meant at least eight fireplaces, possibly more.

Master bedroom. There were two bedrooms that could have qualified. She found the right room, with its dark mahogany furniture uncovered, a folded-up piece of cream-colored cloth on the bed. The quilt.

Kelly set her tote bag on the bed and took out some gloves. As if the oil from her fingertips would cause any more damage to this poor, tattered, sewn mass of patches. Dirt, the age of years, and what looked to be singes from a fire—all qualified this work for the rag bag. Yet someone, namely the head of Firstborn Holdings, LLC, had sent her a request for a bid to restore the neglected and abused fabric.

"All you need is a little love and careful handling," she said aloud, her voice echoing in the room. The folded-up layers of fabric needed to be inspected, inch by inch, which meant Kelly needed to find a place to spread out the quilt. Somewhere with better lighting than the bedroom. One of the inner shutters that covered the windowpanes effectively blocked out the sunlight, but even with both shutters open, the light wouldn't nearly be enough.

She should have ventured enough small talk to ask Mrs. Acres if the electricity was connected in the vacant whaling captain's mansion. She tried a light switch. Nothing. Downstairs there was likely a dining room and a table, with better natural light. Kelly refolded the quilt, then grabbed her tote bag and headed downstairs.

Time to see what was behind those double pocket doors. With the quilt tucked under one elbow, Kelly tugged on the right door. It groaned and complained as it slid on its track but disappeared as it entered the pocket in the wall. A living room, with more furniture draped with sheets, covered by a room-size wool carpet, Persian if she was correct on the pattern. Now *that* was something worth restoring. But then she'd need a studio to do that, and staff willing to help her. The woven pattern was the height of interior decoration at its time, its Middle Eastern influences apparent. Had the owner of the house purchased it on one of his expeditions, or traded for it in some exotic port of call?

Diagonally across the room lay another set of pocket doors, so Kelly headed for those, and slid one of them open. Pay dirt.

A mahogany dining room table ran the length of the space and could comfortably sit sixteen diners. Its flat surface would be ideal to inspect the quilt, and a quartet of windows would give plenty of light. Kelly arranged the quilt on the table before she opened the shutters to let some sunlight into the room, taking care not to let the light fall directly onto the old fabric waiting for her on the table.

She removed her notebook and pen from her tote bag, along with a measuring tape. Yes, this was the first real nibble of work she'd had since the disaster with the Boston Fine Arts Museum. Maybe if she got this bid, the owner might want the other textiles in the home seen to as well. Maybe she could scrounge up a few interns to help her for free, if they'd be brave enough to put her name on their résumé.

The frayed binding told her that the quilt was mere stitches away from disintegrating. When she stepped back and looked at the whole design, she saw the classic Mariner's Compass pattern. The design made her smile. How appropriate for New Bedford. Gray House was situated on County Street, close to the historic district of the former whaling capital of the world. The rays of five compasses spread out from five points on the quilt's field. The muted hues of the diamond-shaped blocks that made the compass patterns told her that someone had used this quilt quite a lot in its day.

She took out her telephone and punched in the number for the contact she had at Firstborn Holdings, a Mr. William Chandler. A voice mail message answered.

"Mr. Chandler, this is Kelly Frost of Frost Textile Services. I'm at Gray House in New Bedford and I'm looking at the quilt. I need to know more information about it, if you could find out for me. Where was it stored? Has anyone else ever worked on it? Please call me back when you have a few moments and I'll give you all my questions."

She set down her phone and continued inspecting the piece. One edge of the quilt, the one frayed and pulling away from the binding, had an uneven edge. Burn marks. Had someone tried to burn it once? The batting had all but disintegrated.

Maybe she didn't need to know the entire history of the quilt, but if some "helpful" person had tried gluing it or using the wrong thread to hold it together, she needed to know that. She continued assessing the quilt and making notes, along with taking digital photographs that she could refer to later. From there she'd tally the sum of her restoration services and give William Chandler and his cohorts an estimate of services.

She pulled out her camera and photographed the quilt section by section, zooming in on some particularly troubled areas. If someone saw this rumpled up cloth in a pile, it would appear ready for the ragbag.

A shadow passed by one of the windows. Kelly jumped. No one could enter the yard except through the iron gate, or unless they hopped the wall-like fence of bricks almost five feet tall that surrounded the property. Or could they indeed hop the fence? She set down her pen.

Then a man's face appeared in the next window. Dark eyes with furrowed dark brows, topped by unruly hair. Kelly bit back a scream. The face disappeared. Another one entered her mind's eye.

*Kelly Frost, you good-for-nothing piece of trash. Get your hind end out of the house and into the garage.*

She clutched at her throat as she struggled to breathe. She hated being jumpy. Her former staff of workers knew better than to sneak up behind her as she worked. No one ever dared to hide behind doors or jumped out and said "boo." That resulted in spilled coffee.

Kelly snatched up her phone. Should she dial 911? Or was that too drastic? Mrs. Acres? She would know if someone had access to the grounds. The front door banged open. The phone slipped from Kelly's fingers and hit the woven rug with a thump.

⸺⸻⸺

Tom Pereira winced as the front door struck the chair rail in the entryway. He hadn't intended the large bang that followed. Well, maybe he had. If there was some punk in this house squatting, Tom could deal with them. Unless they were armed. He hadn't thought about that before charging into Gray House. His responsibility was the grounds and exterior, not the interior.

The place smelled like old people and dust, and Tom tried not to cough.

"Whatever you're doing in here, I can have the boys of New Bedford on the doorstep this side of three minutes," he called out. Okay, so that was probably an overstatement on his part. "So get out here and tell me what's going on."

One of the pocket doors to the front parlor was open. The sound of rustling fabric came from beyond. "Did you hear me? In case you didn't know, I push one button and the cops are here."

He strode across a fancy, ancient rug and through another set of pocket doors and stopped in the doorway separating the parlor from the dining room.

A figure with hair the color of pale sunlight with golden undertones stood beside the immense dining room table. "Same here, whoever you are." She held a cell phone in one hand, her thumb at the ready. Her glare could freeze the harbor water.

"How'd you get in here?"

"Just like you. Through the front door." The young woman stuck her chin out. "I have business here. Mrs. Acres at the property management office let me in."

Tom backed off. No one had told him someone was going to access the house today. But then, they didn't have to. He was only maintenance and groundskeeping, exterior of the building issues only. "All right, then. What kind of business?"

"Why is it your business to find out mine?" Her gaze didn't flinch from meeting his eyes.

He stepped forward, extending his hand. "We're starting off all wrong here. I'm Tom Pereira. I work for the owner of the house. Lawn work, landscaping, the greenhouses, outdoor maintenance. I saw someone inside, didn't know you were coming. Mrs. Acres didn't mention it."

**17**

She set her phone down on the dining table. "Kelly Frost." They shook hands. Her fingertips had calluses. Tom glanced down at her slim hands. "Frost Textile Services. I've been invited to make a bid on restoring this quilt, sewn by Captain Gray's wife. Mrs. Acres brought me here so I can inspect the quilt on-site and then write up my recommendations."

"I'm sorry I scared you."

"You didn't scare me." But her posture when he entered the room told him she was lying. She blinked at him, her icy expression thawing a few degrees.

"Anyway, I'll let you get back to your work. I'll be outside if you need anything." He retreated toward the open pocket doors, trying not to clomp his work boots on the parquet floor.

"Thanks." She turned her attention back to the fabric spread across the dining room table. Tom watched her long enough to see her right hand tremble as she reached for the old fabric. She clenched her hand into a fist.

Back outside in the sunshine, Tom took a deep breath. The longer he worked at Gray House, the more questions he had about its absent owner. When a guy needed work and the perfect job opening came up, he didn't ask questions. Snow plowing the driveway and clearing the sidewalks and roof during the winter had turned into repairing holes in the stone walls surrounding the historic property, then fixing the leak in the koi pond in the backyard. All this attention, for a house no one lived in or used, that he knew of.

But then, Tom didn't care, really, as long as his money was deposited the first of each month into his account. The job was an answer to prayers that he'd bombarded heaven with ever since his discharge from the military. No crowds, no office politics. Just a chance to get his hands dirty and get paid for it.

Nonetheless, he punched the number on speed dial for Mrs. Acres's office. "Yes, uh, this is Tom Pereira. I'm at Gray

House. There's a lady here looking at a quilt. I'm wondering what that's all about."

"I'm sorry, Mrs. Acres is out at the moment," said the female voice on the other end of the phone. "I really don't know anything about the Gray House account. It's restricted."

"Restricted?"

"Mrs. Acres said only she handles this account, so I leave it to her."

"I see. Well, if you could please have her call me when she returns to the office."

"I'll do that, Mr. Pereira."

He was left staring at his phone. Tom shook his head, then clipped his phone onto his belt. There was plenty enough to do outside, like trimming the rosebushes and pruning back the hedges. He ought to mention to Mrs. Acres that the side porch would likely need painting, and possibly a few of the planks replaced. One of three porches, this one faced the side closest to the driveway. It wrapped around the side of the house and ended at the old carriage house at the rear of the property.

Funny, after not quite six months, he'd developed an attachment to the grand old house, almost like a fondness for a great-aunt. An elegant lady, but a little rough around the edges. With love and attention, she'd be back to her prime.

Maybe that's why the pretty stranger had come. Someone had taken an interest in the interior of the building—at long last. He didn't envy them the tasks that awaited. Textiles were the least of the issues inside.

Tom paused at the dining room window where he'd first glimpsed Kelly. She sat hunched over the quilt, her nose inches from the fabric. She scribbled some notes, then sat up. Tom continued along before she caught him. That's all he'd need, getting branded a stalker by someone he barely knew. Maybe he was a stalker, preferring to watch from a distance.

Most days, he didn't feel disabled. Thirty-one was too young to be medically discharged from the Army. But when your coping skills weren't the best and your back had more metal in it than a hardware store, thirty-one was plenty old enough.

Tom hopped off the porch and headed for the greenhouse. He'd known next to nothing about planting, but he figured getting fresh blooms started wasn't that hard. His phone warbled. Mom.

"Hey, Ma."

"Tommy, you going to be home for supper tonight? Nick and Angela are coming with the kids. Plus Bella's arriving soon, toting all her junk home from the university."

"Sure, why not?" He regretted his tone immediately.

"It's been three weeks. A mother wants to see her son sometimes, especially living in the same town."

He felt the sensation of a noose around his neck. "I know, I'm sorry." There'd be three hours of seeing yet again how far he'd fallen short in his father's eyes. Comparisons with Nick, and now even his baby sister Isabella, finishing her freshman year at UMass.

"See you at six, then?"

"I'll be there." He paused. "Love you, Ma."

"I love you too, Son."

Tom ended the call. Family reminded you of what you'd done right and didn't let you forget where you'd gone wrong. He let out a pent-up breath. *Lord, give me strength.*

# 2

Kelly selected the next digital photo, then increased the size. "I'm looking at photo number 40, 125 percent magnification. It looks like silk thread, but I'm not sure. It could also be cotton. What do you think?" She knew the answer, but for old times' sake thought she'd quiz her former intern.

"Um, it sort of does look like cotton to me," said Willa. "But the density is different. I say it's silk. Depending on which sections you choose, it seems like whoever sewed this used two different kinds of thread."

"Good job, you're right." Kelly sighed. "Willa, I wish you could join me on this one, should I get the contract. It's one of the biggest items I've ever bid on. For its size, it's going to need a lot of work."

"I'll work for nothing."

"You can't risk your career by working for me, even for free," Kelly said. "You're going to make an awesome conservator. No, you already are."

"Thanks, Kelly." Willa's voice was warm. "I learned so much from you that one semester."

"Which is why I want you to go on to big things. But I really wanted you to see these photos. There's old glue—I can't imagine who would have tried to glue this quilt, or why. Plus the burn marks."

"What do they want you to do?"

"They want me to make this into a usable quilt, and I can't see how that can happen. Not realistically. There's no way I can restore this to how it used to be. I'll be doing well just to keep it from disintegrating further."

"Well, thanks for calling me about this. I'm honored that you did. I won't say anything to anyone that you're bidding on this job, either."

"Thank you. I have no idea who else is trying for this job. But I need it." She didn't want to tell Willa how badly she needed this quilt job. She'd had to cross her fingers that her credit card would be accepted at the New Bedford Inn.

"I'll be praying that you get it."

"Thanks, Willa." Kelly ended the call, then resumed poring through the photographs she'd taken earlier that day, plus comparing the photos to her notes. This job could save more than her bank account.

She blinked, then stood and stretched. Hours at the computer had snuck up on her. She paced the room a bit, flexing her arms and bending her knees.

What a pretty hotel room. Under other circumstances, she'd have enjoyed the time in the historical setting, with the colonial features and elegant wood trim. She thought of the one-bedroom rented townhouse that waited for her back in Haverhill, over two hours north from here. She hadn't thought about the commute to New Bedford or figuring out the logistics of this quilt job. Surely she'd be able to take it back to her studio, which currently amounted to her bedroom, with her sleeping on her own couch after losing her office space.

Then she shivered again, recalling the guy at the window today, who'd showed up banging the door wide open and scaring up ghosts she'd long since silenced. Or thought she had.

Get a grip. He wasn't Jenks and she wasn't anyone's punching bag anymore, verbal or otherwise. Calming breaths, calming breaths. Of course, he assumed she was an intruder and had come on forcefully. She didn't blame him.

Her heart rate slowed and the shivers fled. She moved back to the desk and the neat rows of prints she'd picked up at the drugstore's photo lab.

What a find, this quilt. Logic screamed that unless this tattered scrap of patches with a pattern that formed five compasses had some strong sentimental value attached to it, spending in the low five figures to restore it was frivolous.

The series of photos reiterated the extent of the damage and neglect the quilt had withstood over the years. One close-up view of a corner made her look carefully at photo 35. Kelly held the photo up and squinted.

Then she set the photo down. She could zoom in with her computer software. She sank onto the cushioned desk chair and scrolled through the images she'd uploaded earlier from her camera. Photo 35.

She zoomed in to the upper left-hand corner, close to the tattered binding of the quilt not far from some scorch marks. She hadn't imagined it. Tiny stitches, the same color as the original background fabric. Creamy white. *With love always for Steban.*

Interesting. Kelly sat up straighter and rubbed her eyes. Some early seamstresses would "write" dedications on the edges of the quilt, but this one was more hidden. Who would write a dedication without it being more obvious?

The quilt had lain inside the house for decades. Maybe Mrs. Acres would know more about it, how long it had been on that bed and why it had been left in such disrepair for so long.

"Focus, Kelly," she said aloud inside the inn's small, snug bedroom. She didn't need to know the answers to those questions to formulate her estimate for the repair bid. The pictures in front of her, plus her notes, told her plenty enough. Some questions didn't need answers. Not yet.

⁂

In the old days, the louder a Pereira gathering was, the better. Tom sat on his motorcycle as dusk fell outside his parents' house. A few extra vehicles had taken up spots in the driveway, like homing pigeons gathered to roost after long journeys.

He'd removed his helmet but still straddled the bike. Tonight, the uproar would grate on his nerves, much like a brood of yapping Chihuahuas around his ankles. But he couldn't swat anyone and tell them no, be quiet.

Tom shifted his weight to his left leg and slung his right leg across the back of the motorcycle, then popped the kickstand. This was his family, his *familia*, where he should feel the safest and be most comfortable. Safety and comfort. He shook his head as he tucked his helmet under his arm.

As he took the steps to the porch, two figures banged open the screen door. "Uncle Tom!"

"Who in the world are you two?" he said to the boy and girl that flung their arms around him.

The oldest child, a boy, laughed. "You know me. I'm Hunter."

"And I'm Hailey," the little girl said.

He kissed them both on the tops of their heads. "But you're too tall. You were shorter the last time I saw you."

"Christmas was a long time ago, Uncle Tom," Hailey said matter-of-factly. "Mom said almost five months. I growed an inch."

"I almost didn't recognize you." He pulled open the screen door, and his niece and nephew scampered inside behind him.

Hunter tugged on his arm. "What does 'Uncle Tom time' mean?"

"Ha!" Tom let out a chuckle. "It means I don't use a clock like everybody else does."

"How do you know when to go places if you don't use a clock?" Hailey's big brown eyes were serious.

"I just know, Miss Hailey, I just know." Tom glanced at Hunter. "And I do use a clock."

Music pounded from behind a closed door upstairs. Bella, home after the spring semester. How times had changed. His parents would have never let him leave the dining room if people were still at the table.

Laughter rang out from the dining room, lined with wood paneling. The craftsman-style home was Pop's pride and joy. Little had changed since Tom left home for the Army thirteen years before, fresh out of high school. How much about him had! No wonder the idea of Uncle Tom time had crept into his life. The house reminded him of everything he'd left behind and of everything that had changed, especially him.

"I was wondering when you'd get here." His mother enveloped him in a hug. "Come on, there's plenty of *chanfana* to eat." She gestured to the sideboard, a carved elegant fixture that had held tons of food over his parents' nearly thirty-five years of marriage. There still remained a giant covered Dutch oven that contained his mother's favorite stew.

"About time you got here." Nick rose and clapped him on the arm. "Good to see you."

"Hey, Tom," said his sister-in-law, Angela.

"Hi, everyone." All faces brightened, except for his father's. Pop looked down at his empty plate with a leftover puddle of gravy from his mashed potatoes.

The two little leeches that had met him at the door followed him to the sideboard. They chattered the entire time about school, about the pair of puppies they'd gotten at Christmas and how the dogs were "going everywhere" inside the house if people didn't let them out in time, and about how they could hardly wait for school to get over with.

"You okay, Tom?" his sister-in-law, Angela, said at his elbow. "These two will talk your ears off if you're around them for long."

"I'm fine. I don't mind listening." That wasn't entirely the truth, but he knew that pushing his own personal preferences aside for family was the right thing to do. He might regret it later, but nothing that a long ride on the bike or a good hike wouldn't cure. The kids didn't know any better, and before he knew it they'd both be grown up and uninterested in the old people. Old in their eyes, like he'd be in about ten years or so. He'd best enjoy their worshipful chatter now.

"Uncle Tom, did you hear us?" Hunter poked his arm. "You seem a million miles away."

Female laughter exploded in the room, both mother and grandmother. "Wherever did you hear that? A million miles away . . ." Angela tousled Hunter's hair.

"He sounds forty, not ten," Mom said, shaking her head.

"A million miles away? Nah." Tom shrugged as he placed some chanfana on his plate. "I was thinking of when you and Hailey will be grown up."

"That's a long time away, Uncle Tom." Hunter pulled a carrot stick from the vegetable tray and crunched down.

"Oh hush." Angela helped herself to a celery stalk. "It's sooner than you realize."

"That's right, kids," Nick called to them. "Before you know it, you'll be as old as me and your Uncle Tom here."

"I can't wait." Hunter plopped onto his chair. "In ten years I'll be twenty. Like Aunt Bella."

"I'll be . . ."—Hailey counted on her fingers—"fifteen."

Tom piled one of his mother's homemade rolls on top of the heap. He took the closest vacant seat next to Nick. "Wow, that's really old."

"I'm going to be in college," Hunter announced.

"That's the plan, buddy," Nick said. "He's already talking about a major."

"At ten? That'll change." Tom took a generous bite of the stew. He wasn't sure what the special occasion was that Mom had cooked up the Portuguese dish, but he wasn't going to complain.

"I'm going to be a paleontologist." Hunter sipped from his cup. "I'm going to unearth a new species." More chuckles from around the table but still silence from Pop. Tom let his gaze slide sideways.

"Hope your college fund is ready for that, Bro," Tom said as he nudged his brother. "That's a long road of education."

"We'll be ready as we can be." Nick smiled across the table at Hunter.

"What did you want to be when you grew up, Uncle Tom?"

The question hung in the air.

"I wanted to be a soldier." He took another bite before he was expected to say more.

"But you're not a soldier no more." Hailey's voice rang out.

"No, not anymore." Reality bit into him once again, in front of the ones who should buoy him up the most. "Hey, Ma, is there fresh coffee in the kitchen?"

"Sure, Tommy. I can get it for you." She shifted on her chair.

"No, I'll get it. Thanks, Ma." He left the table and pushed through the swinging door that separated the dining room from the kitchen.

Of course, his father's unspoken disapproval rang out. No, his crash and burn in the armed forces wasn't his fault. A myriad of things that could go wrong, did. Sort of like the sinking of the *Titanic*.

"Go to college," he'd been told after his medical discharge. The thought of being in a classroom with kids ten years younger than him, the self-absorbed generation that they were, grated on his nerves.

He poured a cup of coffee and inhaled the aroma. Nothing beat a good strong cup of Dunkin Donuts coffee. The fluorescent light over the kitchen sink buzzed, the sound covered up by more laughter from the dining room.

The door creaked open behind him. "Ah, Tommy . . ."

He turned around. "Ma."

"It seems like you and Nick were right around Hunter and Hailey's age, and now look at you." She carried a stack of plates to the counter.

"Here, I'll take care of these." Tommy turned on the faucet and took the plates from his mother.

"But thirty-one . . . you're still so young . . ." His mother pulled open the dishwasher door. "Your father . . . he's old school. He doesn't understand there are many ways to get where you want to be."

That was precisely the problem. He didn't know where he wanted to be.

—⟨⟩—

The old man's chest rose and fell as a tube supplied life-sustaining oxygen to the figure lying on the bed. Earlier that day, the visiting physician had recommended that hospice come in and evaluate the old man for comfort measures.

"Do whatever you think is best to keep him comfortable," he had said to the doctor. The old man protested, just once.

"Is she there, at the house?" the old man asked.

"She was. We're expecting her bid at any time," he replied. "If you're sure she's the one . . ."

"She is." The two words held a bite that made him glance at the old man. "She is."

"Say what you will, but my responsibility is to protect your interests." His own words surprised him.

"My interests are not long for this earth." The old man's voice resumed its normal placid tone.

"You've said that for years."

"I've had to. My interests are all I have left."

# 3

Kelly clicked the send button on the e-mail and shot the bid for the quilt project into cyberspace. Either she would score the biggest job of her shaky career or she'd just committed career suicide. In her written report, she was honest about the damage to the quilt and what would be necessary to keep it from disintegrating further. She determined not to sell herself short, either, so as not to be accused of underbidding.

Her cell phone warbled. She glanced at the number and tried not to roll her eyes. Jonna Spivey, her rival, her nemesis. What now? "Jonna, hello."

"Kelly. I heard you're at the south shore right now." Her voice sounded silken, smooth as cream. "I'm in Newport, Rhode Island."

"Ah, right down the road. You're working on a job, I take it."

"Yes. Just landed a job that'll keep me and my staff occupied through next year. A tapestry collection. You should see the faded threads and the polyester someone used to patch the wool. We're scheduling transport of the first item to the workshop."

Small talk, huh? Of course, there was more to the call today than keeping in touch. Jonna wasn't a colleague who liked to "keep in touch." Jonna was still probably blistering with anger over the last job she'd lost out to Kelly.

"So what are you up to this far south? Your studio hours away."

*Be wise as a serpent* . . . the phrase from the Bible came to her mind. "I'm checking out a prospect. I'm only in town for a few days." She wanted to add, *You're safe from me*, but thought better of it.

"I see. Well, do everyone a favor and don't undercut the bid. Cheapest isn't the best in our industry, but I suspect you know that." The words nipped at her across the airwaves.

"Of course, cheapest isn't the best. Look, I hope you enjoy that new contract of yours. I really need to go."

"Bye, Kelly." The phone went silent.

Kelly allowed herself a sigh. Textile conservators were a unique lot. There were the divas, the self-appointed authorities like Jonna Spivey who saw themselves as the queen bees of a small hive. Then there were the free spirits, like Kelly. They worked alone or in small groups, employing interns and graduate student volunteers, to help shepherd the next generation of conservators. Both had the same goal but had very different ways of reaching it.

Who was she kidding? Free spirit. Lone wolf was probably more accurate. If she got this job, she'd be paid handsomely for her work. Twenty grand would help a lot. But she'd have to do this one alone.

She quit ruminating and rose from the desk chair and went to the window. Instead of checking for new e-mail every five minutes, she ought to take a walk by the harbor. The ocean breeze and call of the gulls used to soothe her as a child. She'd been so busy lately that she hadn't taken time at the waterfront.

The Lord knew what He was doing by creating so much ocean. Probably He knew the world would need a lot of soothing.

Kelly was in her car and heading for the historic district and the harbor front before she reasoned herself out of it. Yes, maybe the free-spirit tag fit. She had no one to claim her time, no one to answer to except God above. She should be thankful.

She angled her car into an empty parking spot and watched as another car passed on the cobblestoned street. Nice, how New Bedford maintained the charm in its historic district. The city had a lot of history, though she had her rough edges. Kelly chuckled to herself and kicked a wayward shell on the pier. So did Haverhill, so did most cities with their mixture of good and evil.

Her phone buzzed. She almost jumped and dropped the phone. But it wasn't a call. Instead, a calendar reminder set for twelve noon, May 5. Lottie's birthday. Lottie was turning sixty today, Lottie who had given Kelly her first sewing machine when she was twelve and allowed her to sequester herself in the junk room of the five-bedroom house that brimmed with foster children. She owed Lottie so much more than sharing a slice of birthday cake with the sweet woman. A phone call wasn't nearly enough.

The breeze cut through her jacket, so she made her way up a couple of blocks from the harbor. A few shops lined the street. A carved wooden sign swung above one storefront, Soup Nation. Someone opened the door, and a swirl of scents drifted onto the sidewalk.

Kelly's stomach growled. She'd skipped breakfast while making the final touches on her bid that morning. She entered and inhaled the mouthwatering aroma. Someone had just pulled a loaf of bread from the oven, too.

She ordered half a grilled cheese panini and a bowl of the fresh tomato soup, then slid into an empty booth. The tiny restaurant enveloped her with its warmth as she sipped her soup and enjoyed the tang of the cheese sandwich. Lottie would greet her with a grilled cheese sandwich after school, once she and the posse of kids walked from the school bus.

Kelly lifted her soup as if in a silent toast, then set it on the table in front of her. A whoosh of air made her look up as the door opened.

The curly-haired grouch from the other day stood in the doorway. He stopped when their gazes collided. He nodded at her.

"Hey," he said as he passed by on his way to the counter.

She returned his nod. Mrs. Acres had apologized all over herself the other day for not telling Kelly about Tom Pereira. Kelly said it wasn't a bother, just a few tense moments. A few tense moments. Ah, she dealt with her own demons enough that she didn't allow them to drift into the forefront of conversations. Playing poor alone-in-the-world Harry Potter never appealed to her, either.

"So, is it going to live?" Tom Pereira asked when he stopped by her table.

"Is what going to live?" She looked up at him and blinked.

"The quilt or whatever you were there to look at the other day."

"Ah, the quilt. I hope so. I won't know for sure, unless I get the bid."

"Bid, huh? If you get the job, we'll have the same boss."

"Firstborn Holdings, LLC, and the elusive Mr. Chandler?" He'd not responded to any of her phone calls about the quilt, except for a terse e-mail requesting the bid before any discussion took place.

He nodded. Then he gestured to the other side of the booth. "Mind if I sit for a minute while I wait on my order?"

"Um, no. Go right ahead." Although she'd planned to enjoy her lunch in silence, Tom would only be there a few moments. In better daylight, she realized he was younger than he'd seemed the other day, closer to her age. His eyes looked tired with tiny lines around the edges, but their warm brown tone looked guarded yet curious. He folded his callused hands on top of the table.

"I'm down here working on another job today. You won't tell Mr. Chandler, will you?" A light entered his eyes.

"Of course not. I might not hear from him anyway. Besides, if there's anything I've learned, sometimes you've got to do what you've got to do, just to get the bills paid." She shrugged and wiped her lips with a napkin.

"That's so very true. So . . . what in the world does a textile conservator do, exactly?"

"We repair and restore old fabrics. I've worked on every-thing from vintage clothing to samplers to medieval tapestries. Most of the time, though, I spend time repairing backfired attempts to patch a piece together." Ah, here she went, yam-mering about her job. His eyes weren't quite glazing over, so she figured she'd quit while she was ahead.

"I see."

Of course, he didn't see. But that was fine by her. "So, how long have you worked for Mr. Chandler and company?"

"About six months. They needed someone to help with snow removal over the winter, and I needed the job." His gaze drifted over her shoulder and in the direction of the counter. "My order's up. Good talking to you."

"Same here." She turned her focus back to her cooling soup as Tom stood and headed for the counter. Handsome. A bit unpolished. Moody. Not her type at all. Yet, her type had left her heart with a gash that had taken far too long to heal.

Tom passed by her booth on his way from the counter, carrying a cardboard container stacked with sandwiches and covered cups of soup. He didn't acknowledge her. If she got the job, she might see him again. If not, yet another stranger passing through her life.

*God, if you're listening . . .* She stopped her silent prayer. Ever since she'd come to New Bedford, a restlessness had bitten into her with slow nibbles. It had to be that today was Lottie's birthday. That, or the fresh reminder that she was between jobs.

*. . . I need something to change, but I don't know what.* The sunlight streaming in the wall of windows warmed her, but she fought the shiver that wanted to come.

Her phone buzzed . . . William Chandler. Her pulse rate shot up into the stratosphere. "This is Kelly Frost."

"Ms. Frost, William Chandler with Firstborn Holdings. The CEO has reviewed your bid and accepted it. The Gray House job is yours."

"Thank you, thank you!" She tried to modulate her voice, but the words came out in a quaver.

"I've e-mailed you further details, but you may pick up your key from Mrs. Acres at the management company and move in on June one."

"Move in?"

"Nothing is to be removed from the house. All work will be completed on site."

She fought for the right words. He could yank the bid away from her if she flubbed her response. Nothing had been signed yet . . . but moving to New Bedford? Not that she had anything to tie her to Haverhill, but—

"Ms. Frost?"

"Yes. I'll be looking for that e-mail."

"You don't have a problem working on-site?"

"I . . . I honestly hadn't anticipated that. But, you're sending more details in an e-mail?"

"Yes, including an agreement which must be signed and notarized and overnighted to our offices within seven days or you will forfeit the contract."

"I understand. I'll be in touch."

The line went dead. Moving to New Bedford, even temporarily for up to four months? How would she find a place to live that fit her skinny budget? But then Mr. Chandler had mentioned something about moving in? Moving *into* Gray House? The place was creepy, even in the daytime.

---

"You took long enough getting lunch," Mac leaned on the pickup truck in front of the house they were roofing not two blocks from the café.

"Soup Nation, made to order. You wanted the chowder, and it wasn't done yet." Tom set the cardboard tray of food on the truck hood. "So here it is."

"Well, we need to eat fast. Lenny's going to be back in fifteen minutes, and we'll finish this job today." Mac grabbed the nearest container of fresh chowder and a plastic spoon. "Rain's coming in tonight, so we've gotta get a move on."

Tom nodded. "Thanks for calling me about this job. I'm ready anytime you need a hand." He didn't want to sound desperate, but if he could get in full time with a good contractor, maybe he could quit the Gray House job.

"That's the thing . . . I was going to tell you later, but not when Lenny's here. Might as well do it now." Mac set his soup down on the truck and rubbed his forehead. "I hate to say it, but I won't need your help after this job's over, probably not for a while."

"You won't?" Tom tried not to show it, but shock jolted through him like electricity. Couldn't a guy ever get a break?

"No, I'm cutting back on my helpers. I've got to cut costs somehow." Mac put his hand on Tom's shoulder. "You're the last one I hired."

"I understand." Sure, he understood Mac's reasoning. But he didn't like it one bit.

"Maybe if I can find a way to cut costs, I could ask you back. But I don't see how."

Tom nodded. He wanted to sling his sandwich into the street and just leave, go anywhere. But he'd done that before and burned at least one bridge to a final crisp.

"I'll pay you your cut today, even though I haven't seen the rest of my own payment."

"Thanks." *Thanks for nothing, for four weeks' worth of jobs . . .*

"You still have your other job, the outdoor caretaker?"

"Yeah, I do."

"I bet you're getting a lot of experience with that one."

"Here and there. Mostly landscaping right now." And he wasn't even the gardening type, either. But Chandler had told him to tend the roses while he was at it. "Not much of a green thumb, either." He chuckled at the irony.

"Maybe God's pushing you out of your comfort zone," said Mac.

"Maybe." If Mac knew anything about him, he considered comfort a friend who'd deserted him a long time ago.

# 4

Lottie, I got a new contract." Kelly stood on one side of the sales counter and fidgeted with the packets of needles arranged in a symmetrical pattern by the register. Threads by Lottie had become a fixture in Haverhill, as had Kelly's former foster mother. Lottie had always dreamed of having a shop. As Kelly's dream had sprouted, so had Lottie's.

The gray-haired woman rose from the chair at the desk. "Kelly . . . it's been too long."

"I thought I'd say hello before I left town. I put some of my things in storage, but I'm heading out now." She hated the apologetic tone in her voice. In the same town, she could have gone by Lottie's, either the shop or the old house. But she hadn't.

Busy, she always said. Fostered out, reality told her. Lottie had never turned her to the curb like some foster parents did when their children turned eighteen, but a sense of being on the outside, always, nudged Kelly away from the warm circle that was life in Lottie and her husband, Chuck's, home. A gaggle of foster kids stair-stepped in ages had been her brothers and sisters for the final six years she was in the system. Her first six years had been seared from her memory.

"Leaving, are you?" Lottie leaned on the counter. She acted as if she wanted to round the corner and give Kelly a hug but thought better of it.

"New Bedford, at least through September, maybe October."

"Right on the coast. Beautiful."

"Contract says I need to live in Gray House while I work on my project. Nothing like living in an old mansion. Poor me." Kelly laughed, but Lottie didn't smile.

"You be careful down there." Lottie rubbed her arms and shivered. "Just knowing you've been here in town, knowing you're all right . . ."

"I'll be fine. Besides, living on-site will save me rent. Good thing my lease is month to month here anyway." She grinned at Lottie. "I'll call you, or e-mail you. You *are* using e-mail, aren't you?"

"I know how to e-mail." Lottie returned the grin, her expression lighting up her face. "Don't be shocked, but Threads has a website, too. I'm not getting on the Facebook and Twitter stuff, though."

"You do what you think is best, really." Kelly patted Lottie's hand, soft and slightly wrinkled. "I know that Facebook can be a great marketing tool, but even I'm not to that point yet." Willa had tried to talk her into it once, and had nearly succeeded until Kelly got a freaky friend request from a stranger who was "enchanted with her photograph." That spurred her into deleting her account.

"Make sure you call me, please, or something, and give me updates." Lottie almost sounded as if she were pleading. "I always like making sure my kids are okay."

"I will. I promise." Kelly watched as Lottie ambled around the counter. She closed her eyes as Lottie embraced her. The closest thing to a real mother she ever had, yet somehow it never seemed enough.

After another good-bye and another promise to keep in touch, Kelly scurried from the shop and out to her car that fairly groaned with all her supplies and sundries. Two hours later, plus an extra half hour getting through a snarl in Boston traffic, she breathed a little easier. Good-bye, Haverhill. Good-bye to what she'd known for most of her adult life.

The closer she'd gotten to the coast, the more clouds piled up along the western horizon. A storm system drifting across the area. New Bedford greeted her with a bleak, gray sky. How fitting, given that she was now pulling up in front of Gray House. Wait. Mrs. Acres had said the back gate had a keypad and that she should take her car inside the perimeter of the property.

A motorcycle sat crosswise on the slab that made up two parking spaces, leaving her no choice but to pull onto part of the lawn. Dark, tousled hair Tom what's-his-name would probably object to her parking, but if he was the owner of the motorcycle, he was to blame.

Her car sputtered to a stop, then the engine coughed and died. Well, she wasn't about to go anywhere, anyhow. Although she probably should have stopped to pick up a few groceries. The idea had escaped her during her enthusiasm about the new project. She still shook her head, that her bid was accepted. It wasn't the lowest, but she still marveled that someone would pay the kind of price to have a mere bed covering restored.

A few raindrops spattered on the ground as Kelly exited the car, lugging her laptop and her suitcase into the back entrance by the kitchen. Mrs. Acres had given her a key ring with front and back door, plus mailbox keys when she stopped by the property management office.

"There are other locks and cabinets and such in the house, but these are the most important ones you'll need," the older woman had assured her. "You need anything else for the house, call me day or night."

The spatter of rain turned into a brisk downpour by the time she reached the kitchen entrance. Once inside, she shut the door behind her. The sound echoed in the house. Kelly shivered.

She hadn't seen the kitchen on her first visit. White walls, white cabinets, and a large wooden island in the center of the immense room. A high ceiling held a pot rack over the island. Kelly stepped across the black-and-white tile floor. No, this room had been updated at some point and wasn't original to the house. Well, some of it anyway.

The sound of her footsteps and clicking suitcase wheels echoed off the bare walls. The space was so . . . empty of warmth. She shook off the sensation and pushed through the swinging door and found herself in the dining room. Wrong door. She needed to find the main hall and head upstairs to fig-ure out where she was going to sleep. On impulse, she flipped the light switch. The chandelier glowed, casting the reflected lights from hundreds of crystals. Gorgeous now, it must have been breathtaking in the era of gaslights. Kelly turned off the light and headed for the pocket doors she'd used a few weeks ago.

Lightning flashed, followed by a boom of thunder that rattled the windows. Kelly pulled her suitcase along behind her, up the wooden staircase with its curved banister that led to the second floor. She started trying doors. Which room to choose as hers?

The other day, she'd been on a mission to find the quilt that now lay on Captain Gray's bed where she'd found it. Kelly pushed open the first door, a front bedroom that looked out onto County Street. Simply decorated in tones of blue and cream, it had a peaceful air to it. A settee was positioned under the shuttered front window. A good possibility, although perhaps there might be street noise if she left a window open. Or were there rules about opening windows of the historic house?

Kelly laid her laptop case on the bed and let her suitcase down at the corner of the four-poster bed draped with a frilly canopy. Rain drummed on the windows full force now. Kelly flung the shutters open to let pale gray light into the shadowed room.

She moved on to the next bedroom, this one smaller and decorated for a little boy. A few turn-of-the-twentieth-century toys were arranged at the corner of a dark-patterned rug. It was as if the family had left for the weekend and were due back any moment. Kelly moved to the closet and opened the door. Little boys' clothing hung from the rack and a faint whiff of *something* struck her nostrils. Not on the clothes. She leaned closer . . . smoke? But old, very old.

Her nosy meter shot into overdrive. She'd definitely ask Mrs. Acres more about the house once she got settled in. Kelly left the room through a door that connected it to the next room.

This was a lady's room, elegant and dramatic in shades of crimson and gold. Captain Gray's wife's room, perhaps? The maple wood bed rested almost on a dais-like platform with steps. Kelly shook her head. The front room would be more for her.

She entered the hallway again and shivered. Maybe she should see where the thermostat was. Or did the house have more than one? Not in the main hallway.

Kelly stepped across to the other side of the hall to find a study and a seamstress's room. The sewing room made her smile. Maybe she'd make this her sewing room as well, if the light were right.

At the back corner of the house, opposite the captain's room, she found a narrow staircase that led in two directions, one to the kitchen below and the other to the third floor. Her curiosity piqued, she took the creaky steps.

Servants' quarters, simple yet neat. Sparsely decorated with a modest fireplace at each end. An even narrower staircase led the way to the tiptop of the house, the lookout room. Kelly placed her toes on each step, barely meeting the middle of her arch. Yes, people had tinier feet one hundred fifty years ago.

One more turn of the stairs and she emerged into a square room, no larger than four-by-four feet, framed with windows and a low bench that ran the perimeter of the space. Kelly squinted into the pouring rain outside and caught a glimpse of the harbor, blocks away and downhill from County Street.

She could well imagine the captain's wife climbing these stairs every day, watching to see when her husband would return. Kelly looked up at the wooden roof and at the corner trim. A few droplets of water were leaking through the roof and running along a wooden ridge. She ought to tell someone, for the sake of the building.

She placed one knee on the bench and reached up to touch the dampness. As she did so, the bench seat wobbled. This was probably the last place in the house anyone looked at to maintain. Kelly reached for the bench seat and it slid away from the wall.

A metal box lay lengthwise in the recessed seat. Old, very old. Kelly sucked in a deep breath as she pulled out the box, her wrist straining with the unexpected weight. She hefted it onto the edge of the bench and opened the box.

An old leather-bound book lay inside. Someone had taken care to put this away for safekeeping. Kelly opened up the cover. Inside, the faded pages were covered with a flowing script. She needed gloves to look at this further.

She allowed herself to sneak a read of the opening lines.

*February 1850*

*Surely the Lord Himself has smiled upon me, Mary Smith Gray, that He bestows upon me such a situation! Indeed, I am exclaiming for joy. Hiram Gray is my wedded husband. A serious and devout man, but I see a spark within his silvery eyes. A woman ought not to think of nor write of such things. But here on these pages, meant for no other mortal's eyes, I can freely share.*

Kelly closed the cover, glancing around although she was alone. Mary Gray's diary. She returned it to the metal box. This book was important to the house. How long it had been here, she didn't know.

The rain cascaded down the windows in little rivers that blurred the world outside. Kelly shivered again. She needed to take the book downstairs, out of this place and into a more controlled environment.

A flash of color at the door of the greenhouse in the back corner of the immense yard caught her eye. Tom Pereira, wearing a red shirt under a dark jacket. Hopefully, this time Mrs. Acres had told him of her arrival, and her occupation of the house.

Kelly tucked the box under her left arm, holding the priceless cargo close to her side. Heading down was far worse than climbing up stairs meant for someone the size of a child. She managed to negotiate the stairs and soon had the box resting on her bed in the front room.

"Hello?" a male voice called out from below. "Ms. Frost?"

She touched her hair then descended the main staircase. "I'm here . . ." She rounded the corner of the lowest banister just as Tom entered the hallway.

"I moved my motorcycle," he said, water droplets falling from his hair, now starting to curl with the humidity. "If you give me your keys, I can get your car back on the parking spot and off the grass."

"Oh, that would be great. I didn't want to block you in, and then it started raining." She pulled her keys from her jacket pocket and handed them to Tom. "I assume Mrs. Acres told you I was coming."

He nodded. "Congratulations, I think? You're moving into this mausoleum, then?"

"For now." She didn't want to explain to him, but then, she didn't need to. His opinion of her situation didn't matter. He knew nothing about her.

"I'll make sure the first floor of the carriage house has a place for you to park, if you want." He half smiled and for half a second didn't look as if the world's worries had weighed him down.

"Don't go to any extra trouble for me."

"No trouble, not at all." He spun the keys around on one finger and left in the direction of the kitchen.

When he wasn't grouchy, suspecting her of being an intruder, he was pretty good-looking. Kelly followed the path he'd taken. She might as well take stock of what groceries she needed. Once she got in her work zone, she didn't pay much attention to cooking or food. Which reminded her, she needed to gather a collection of takeout menus.

Kelly entered the kitchen and began opening cabinets. Most were empty, save a solitary cabinet that held like-new dishes, enough for four. So her new employer had thought of that much. The vintage refrigerator wasn't even plugged in, she discovered.

Outside, the rain still pounded. Amidst the downpour, Kelly heard the valiant effort of her car's engine to turn over.

Car repairs weren't in her budget. She had half her stipend now, plus the money up front for supplies.

Kelly went to the kitchen window closest to where the drive lay outside. Tom exited her car, and as he did so, he glared at it. She didn't blame him one bit. She moved to the back door and opened it.

"I'm not sure what's wrong with it. I'm just glad it made it all the way from Haverhill," she said.

Tom pulled one of her plastic-covered tote boxes from the backseat. "We'll wait till the rain stops."

She scurried out to meet him. "You don't have to unload my car."

"It's okay. I don't have anything else to do at the moment." He extended the tote in her direction, and she took it from him. He held onto it, making sure she had a good grip, his fingertips brushing hers.

—oeeo—

A man would have to be half-dead not to have felt that electricity. Standing here in the rain, it could have been deadly. Tom tore his focus away from Kelly's eyes and his mind from the sensation of her fingertips. A man would have to be half-blind not to notice her. Not that she stood out from a crowd, but when you let yourself take a second look . . .

"You carry this inside," he told Kelly. "I'll bring the rest of the stuff in. You have more in the trunk, I assume?"

She nodded and turned back toward the open kitchen door, leaving him to wrestle with his thoughts. Not much wrestling took place, actually. He wasn't looking to meet someone, not really. Right now things weren't the best for him. It was all he could do to keep positive, and nobody wanted to be around a guy who slipped into Eeyore mode.

He focused on the mission at hand, getting Kelly's car emptied and her stuff unloaded in the house. As far as what was wrong with it, he'd save that for later. She didn't look like she was in a hurry to go anywhere anytime soon. She had three bags of shoes, plus another uncovered tote with what looked like art supplies. Then a container of books. By the time Tom emptied the trunk, the rain had slowed to a patter.

Once Tom entered the kitchen with the last load, he'd made quite a puddle on the tile floor. The water and mud stood out on the black and white. "Sorry about that."

"Don't worry about it." Kelly's gaze traveled the room. "I assume there must be cleaning supplies somewhere."

"They didn't tell you anything?"

She shook her head. "Just that I had to keep the quilt onsite and that I was welcome to stay in the house for nothing. Other than that, no."

"So you could drop everything and come here."

"This was really my only option right now . . . times have been tough. And this seemed like the answer to my prayers." Kelly shrugged out of her jacket, not quite as soggy as his. "Anyway, I'm here now."

"Well, good for you."

"Is that a little sarcasm I hear?"

"No, not at all. It's a brave move. Do you have family around here?" he asked.

Kelly shook her head. "No. No family." She appeared to study the mud on the floor. "Guess I should get that mud cleaned up."

He nodded. "I should get back to the greenhouse. Our boss has more confidence in my gardening abilities than I do."

"What do they grow here and why, if no one visits or lives here?"

"Rosebushes, for one thing. Over one hundred years old. And, I recently was notified they're going to be not just maintaining the lawn, but giving it a facelift." Tom heard the sound of a car pulling into the driveway. He wasn't expecting anyone. He glanced at Kelly. "Someone's here."

He stepped outside, with Kelly following. He held back a whistle at the sight of the black, high-end SUV now with mud on the tires. The driver killed the engine.

A man emerged from the driver's side of the vehicle. "Ah, so you two have met. I'm William Chandler. You must be Tom Pereira. We've chatted several times over the past few months. And you must be Kelly Frost, just arrived from Haverhill."

Kelly stepped around Tom, extending her hand. "Yes, I'm Kelly Frost. Tom was helping me unload my car."

Chandler nodded. "I apologize for the rather bleak reception. My—the house has been closed up for decades. No one's lived here since the current owner was a young man, at least seventy years ago."

"Well, I'm looking forward to staying here."

Chandler reached inside his jacket pocket. "Here's a prepaid credit card for any miscellaneous items you may need during your stay."

"Wow, thank you." She studied. "This will come in handy."

"Please, let either me or even Mr. Pereira know if there's anything that needs work in the house." At this, Tom snapped to attention. Indoor work now? He'd better get some kind of a raise for these extra jobs that popped up.

"The rain doesn't help much with the atmosphere, but it's a beautiful house inside. It just needs a little attention and TLC, like the quilt." Kelly smiled at Chandler, who reminded Tom of a sly fox. Matter of fact, the guy was a lawyer or something for the owner. It figured. Tom ripped his focus away from Kelly's smile. He didn't picture her as the kind who'd go gaga over a suit. But hey, it happened.

"I hope you'll find the situation here conducive to work," said Chandler. "I tried explaining to my employer that it would probably be better to ship the quilt to your studio, but what can I say? The man's eccentric and wouldn't hear of it leaving the house. He has some idea of restoring the house to its glory days of his childhood."

"I understand. After all, he's the one who asked for bids." Kelly rubbed her bare arms, then shivered. "I'm going to step inside if you don't mind. My jacket's in there."

"Not at all," said Chandler. "I need to speak to Mr. Pereira here privately for a moment."

"All right." Kelly shot Tom a questioning look before taking the steps and heading inside. Tom shrugged. He'd only met Chandler once. No, twice, during his six months at Gray House.

"Mr. Pereira, I want you to know how much Firstborn Holdings appreciates your work. My employer is giving you this." He handed him an envelope. "Just a token of thanks. Another thing." Chandler glanced at the door leading to the kitchen.

"Yes?"

"Watch Ms. Frost. Her company has a good reputation. We've seen samples of her work and she comes highly recommended from one of the best museums in New England. However, there were a few issues of character that gave our CEO pause." Chandler took his own pause, just like a lawyer, for effect.

"Issues, huh?" Tom had enough of his own . . . but "character" issues?

"Enough said." Chandler clapped him on the back. "Please, keep an eye on her. We'll keep in touch."

# 5

By nightfall, Kelly had settled into the front bedroom. A small table for two that sat in front of the pair of windows made an ideal station for her laptop. She'd never stayed in a room this nice, stale air and all. She managed to open one of the windows a crack, but air that entered was humid, so she thought better of that idea and closed the window.

After stumbling along and finding an art deco shower in the bathroom between the master bedroom and the study, Kelly felt half-human and completely warm again in her pajamas. The rain had given her shivers for most of the afternoon. She'd checked her phone and found a Thai place that delivered, not six blocks away.

Thankfully, Mr. Chandler had shown up with the prepaid card. She honestly hadn't been sure about supper or anything until then. This allowed her to at least order some takeout for supper, after Tom had gone along his way.

Weird, that his demeanor had smoothed over until he was as impassive as a brick. He'd almost seemed . . . talkative . . . until Mr. Chandler's arrival.

She sat down at the little table and looked out at the dark night. Lights twinkled on the waterfront, and a few stars crept out now that the clouds had blown away. The pad Thai was spicy and awakened her taste buds. She chased the noodles down with sips of diet soda. Note to self—find a place to walk or jog, or her rear end would expand with all the sitting she was going to do this summer.

Tonight was the perfect time to discover that there was no Internet access at all, save a few unsecured connections, and she didn't feel right accessing those.

In the morning, after she started her preliminary work on the quilt, she'd see if her car would cooperate and head to the store to buy a wireless connection. She'd need it, both to order supplies and contact any of her colleagues who would be willing to answer her questions.

The pad Thai had filled her up, but she didn't feel tired just yet. The house was eerie enough by day. By night? Kelly didn't think she could make it down to the kitchen to brew a cup of tea, were she fortunate enough to find a teapot.

She padded on bare feet over to the metal box on the antique vanity and opened it. Before she pulled it out of the box, she donned a pair of white gloves. Then she allowed herself to carry it over to the window table. Imagine, Mary Gray's journal had lain up there so long, forgotten, like many things had been in this old house.

Kelly sat down, then opened up to the page where she'd been reading.

*But here on these pages, meant for no other mortal's eyes, I can freely share.*

There were a few lines of unintelligible writing, something about having a terrible headache and calling the doctor.

*March 1850*

*We are hosting a ball. I can scarcely believe that my Hiram has allowed it. He has been in such an ill temper that he sounds almost like my father did. Men can be such foul-tempered beasts, no matter how often they go to their knees in prayer. I said as much once to Hiram, and he left a mark on my cheek. No one asked where it came from. I suppose I deserved it for speaking so. He struck me only once this week. I should be grateful and work at holding my tongue.*

Kelly shuddered and closed the journal. Poor lady, starting her journal with high hopes. A marriage to a good, upstanding man. Yet Kelly understood far too well that not all men were as they appeared. A man could claim one thing and still have another layer of truth below the one he paraded before others.

No wonder Mr. Chandler gave her the creeps. He might as well have been Peyton Greaves, with all his luster and polish. Peyton, whose betrayal even now stung and whose kisses and lies had cost her a price she was even now paying. No sirree, Mr. Chandler. His polish didn't fool her, not to the tips of his fancy leather shoes getting wet in the rain this afternoon.

Kelly stood and took Mary Gray's diary back to the metal case. Great. Now she'd probably be awake half the night, and a full day awaited her tomorrow. It was too late to call Lottie. The comfort of her voice would have helped soothe away the jumbled nerves. It would be nice to be able to call her again. Lottie didn't know about Peyton, and Kelly planned to keep it that way. She sat back down at the window and sipped the rest of her soda.

So Mary Gray's husband had hit her, and Mary acted as if that were normal. He likely pretended it didn't happen. But that was in the days long before abuse was talked about.

Peyton had never struck her. Jenks, though, had taught her that men could have that moodiness Mary described in her diary. One minute smiling, the next making her and the other children pay for someone else's transgression.

No wonder she'd fallen hard for Peyton once he'd worn her guard down. Kelly sighed. Every day she prayed that the past would stay firmly in its place. People at her old church spouted the verse about all things being made new for those who are "in Christ." It was easy enough to say things like that if you'd never had anything bad happen and if your worst disappointment was the restaurant being out of blue cheese dressing.

"Don't waste time counting sheep when you can't sleep; talk to the Shepherd," Lottie used to tell the children whenever anyone had a hard time sleeping.

It used to work for her during those six years under Lottie and Chuck's watchful care. She'd whisper away to the unseen Heavenly Father, just as Lottie suggested, and somehow to her teenage soul, the practice was like a balm. Back then, she clung to whatever anchor she could find, and this one worked.

She found her cell phone charger and plugged it into the nearest empty outlet. Surely Mr. Chandler would have mentioned if there was an issue with the electricity, but then again maybe not. She plugged her phone into the charger. One missed call. Lottie. And one new voice mail.

"*Three thirty-five p.m.* Hi, Kelly. It's Lottie. Just wanted to make sure you arrived okay and all's going well. Call me when you get a chance."

Her heart swelled at the sound of Lottie's voice. She set the phone down. As she did so, a floorboard creaked in the hallway, then another. She tiptoed to the bedroom door, then stopped, listening at the door. She yanked it open, only to see an empty hallway filled with moonlight. Silly. There was no one in the house with her except antiques and memories.

Five hundred dollars. It was an odd six-month bonus for a mere outdoor maintenance guy. The weight of the five bills was like a brick in Tom's back pocket as he drove through town the next morning. Sure, who couldn't use an extra five hundred? But it wasn't nice to feel as if the money were a bunch of carrots dangling from a stick, coaxing him along somewhere he wasn't sure he wanted to be.

Maybe it wasn't a big deal. Just in case, though, he'd hang on to the money. He pulled his motorcycle into the parking lot of Patillo's Marina. Mac had called last night, giving him the number of a guy who might have a possible job for him. The guy by the name of Dave Winthrop would meet him at the marina the following morning, aboard the *Peggy Sue*. Evidently he lived on a houseboat and had just bought a townhouse but needed some changes made to the place before his wife would move in.

Hand-to-mouth living, job to job. Tom shrugged off the sensation of scrounging. People should be coming to him, not him going to them, carrying his proverbial hat as if he wanted a handout.

"You can go to college," someone had said. "It'll all be paid for, and then some."

He wasn't college material. High school had been hard enough. Tests made him freeze. Numbers ran together and rearranged themselves on the page. Dyslexia had been easy enough to diagnose, but that didn't make his life easier.

There it was, the *Peggy Sue*, bobbing in place, her sails tied down. A man waited at the edge of the pier.

"Tom Pereira?" the guy called out.

"That's me." Tom ambled along the pier, and shook hands with the man. "My buddy John MacGraw said you needed help with your new townhouse."

"Dave Winthrop. Nice to meet you, and I do need a hand."

"What's wrong with the place?"

"The carpeting's old, and my wife wants hardwood through-out the living areas and tile in the kitchen. Do you have any floor laying or tiling experience?"

"I've worked on my brother's house. We renovated the entire first floor. Also, I've helped John on a few jobs." His brother's floor didn't turn out half-bad, either. He had a good eye for straight lines and occasionally needed to recheck his measurements, but the floor gleamed, as did the travertine in the kitchen.

"Well, I know you have to work today, but can you meet me at the townhouse at five? That way you can take some measurements and hear it straight from my wife's mouth what she wants so you can give us an estimate." Dave squinted out across the water toward the city. "Pereira . . . what nationality is that last name?"

"Portuguese. You'll find a lot of us around here." Tom shrugged. "I'm a mix, though. Italian's in there somewhere along the family tree, too. Grew up here in New Bedford."

"I know the question was a little odd. I'm a genealogy buff. It's sort of a hobby of mine, so I can't help but ask. I traced my father's family back to fourteenth-century England. It took a while, but I now have a framed family tree."

"Wow, that's impressive." Tom hoped that wasn't a lie. He figured their meeting later today would involve a display of the family tree. Not that that kind of thing didn't interest him, it was just strange to find out something like that when first meeting someone.

"Well, I'll see you at five." Dave handed him a card. "Here's the address."

"All right, then, thanks."

He left with a lighter step than he'd had in a while. Maybe this was part of his new start. He could do flooring, and he could do tile. If this project worked out for him, it could be a whole new venture in his life.

By the time Tom got to Gray House, the morning clouds had lifted and he had a ton of work ahead of him. Chandler's request from yesterday niggled at him once again. *Character issues*, he'd said. Tom realized he didn't know much about Kelly Frost. He also realized he'd developed a soft spot for the old whaling captain's house. Although whatever character issues Kelly had, Tom wasn't sure how they could affect her job at Gray House.

Kelly's vehicle was still half on the parking slab, half on the grass. Great, one more thing he'd forgotten. First thing, he'd get her vehicle running, or at least see what the problem was. He killed the motorcycle engine after he'd parked close to the greenhouse. Chandler had asked that he work on some fresh summer plantings to get the gardens back to what they were in their glory days. They could probably wait a few hours longer. They'd waited decades already.

Tom climbed off the bike, then took off his helmet and placed it on the seat. The sooner he got her car running, the sooner he could get back to his own work. He walked up to the kitchen door and pounded. Who knows where she was in the massive old house? He noticed a small button set into the wooden door frame. He pushed, just in case the ancient doorbell worked.

The door flew open. "Good morning." Kelly wore a shirt that had seen better days, with stains and was at least two sizes too large and hid her curves. Her pink toenails peeked out from under the hem of her worn jeans.

"Do you mind if I have your car keys back, so I can pop the hood?"

"Oh, that's right . . . my car. I was getting started on the quilt this morning and the car slipped my mind." She glanced over her shoulder. "I'll grab the keys." She turned and trotted from the kitchen.

Within seconds she reemerged. "Here." She handed him the keys and followed him to her car. "Do you know much about cars?"

"Ah, I've tinkered here and there. I can at least tell you what the problem isn't."

"Well, once you figure out what it is, I need to get a few groceries from the store and essentials, like a coffeepot." She rubbed her forehead. "I think I'm having caffeine withdrawal this morning."

"Ouch." He tried not to chuckle, but he knew what that was like. Once he'd unlocked the car and popped the hood, he tried the first logical thing, the ignition. He noticed the dome light didn't come on when he opened the door.

No life from the battery. "I think it's your battery," he said.

She bit her lip. "Think?"

"I can take it out and run it to an auto supply store so they can test it for you. If it's a dud, I can pick up a new one." An easy fix.

"It figures, once I get here, money starts draining away." Kelly shook her head. "Sorry. I appreciate your help. Do you think fifty bucks ought to do it for a battery? Or should I send more?"

"Fifty is fine to start with. If it ends up being more, I'll take care of it and you can pay me back."

"Thank you, thank you. I'm just trying to keep some kind of a budget here . . . Hang on while I grab some cash." Off she sped again, into the house.

Yes, he definitely knew about keeping a budget. He had a feeling, too, she'd pay him every last cent she owed him, that she kept a strict accounting on what she owed anyone. Pride did that to someone, especially someone wanting to make sure they carved their own way in the world.

Tom fished a wrench out of his tool bag and soon had the battery taken out of Kelly's car and strapped onto his motorcycle. The nearest auto supply store that he knew of was a good fifteen-minute ride away.

Kelly pounded down the steps. "Here." She pressed the money into his hand. "Thanks for helping. I don't know what I would have done if you weren't here."

"You'd have figured something out." He stood there, staring down at her hand that had clamped a folded bill into his palm. "I have a feeling you're that kind of woman."

# 6

The quilt was spread open to its full width and length as it air-dried on a layer of cotton towels. It had taken Kelly three hours of careful, gentle pulls and tugs to get the poor thing washed that morning, braced between layers of netting that could bear the brunt of Kelly's pulls and tugs. Simply lukewarm water in the claw-foot bathtub of the lady's bathroom upstairs, and she'd had to change the water three times.

The idea of washing the quilt terrified her. The whole thing could dissolve into a heap of quilt blocks and threads. There wasn't much she could do right now except wait for the quilt to dry and see what she could start to work on rescuing.

Underneath the soft lights she'd set up on tripods surrounding the quilt, Kelly could see that although much of the surface grime was gone with the gentle washing, there were numerous torn stitches across the entire Mariner's Compass. Every little triangle and block that made up the arms of the five stars had frayed or missing stitches. The binding had nearly fallen apart or disintegrated. Dozens of the triangular quilt blocks, originally hand pieced, were missing from the quilt altogether.

"Mary Gray, your quilt is a wreck, but I promise you, I'll do my best to put it back together again," Kelly said aloud. Truly, the hand stitching made this quilt priceless in the eyes of the right collector. A good number of Kelly's hand stitches would help give new life to the piece.

Tom's words before he'd gone to fetch a new car battery rang in her ears. *You'd have figured something out. I have a feeling you're that kind of woman.*

Yep, he had her pegged right. She wasn't used to having someone there in a pinch. She'd learned to figure things out for herself. After determining the problem was a dead car battery, she'd paid Tom back and he'd disappeared into the greenhouse, leaving her to the quilt, at last.

Kelly yawned. After hearing the floor creak throughout the night, then being awakened by the dawn peeking through an open shutter, she would welcome a nap this afternoon. She sat cross-legged on the tile floor in the bathroom, listening to the gulls call from the harbor.

Her phone remained silent after her voice mail to Mr. Chandler, asking yet again for more information about the quilt. The ink was dry on the contract, but she should have demanded more history about the quilt and its owners before proceeding. Its sorry state should have provided information enough. Plus, she hadn't counted on the whole living-on-site stipulation. The setup was the oddest she'd ever encountered. And yet Mary Gray's journal enticed her from its perch on the bedroom bureau.

The words haunted her even now in the morning light.

. . . *I have accepted my lot with Hiram Gray and know my place. The only troubling of the waters is that he leaves again, and soon. Misdirected and delayed letters that arrive from him shall be the only things I can clasp to my bosom over the next long many months, years. 'Tis the whales that call to him. He must answer, for all the opportunities it gives to us and those who depend on Hiram. He is a good Christian man, of Quaker descent. Not unusual for the sea, but not typical, either. The fact that he should marry me, an orphan with nothing, speaks to his Christian background.*

*Hiram has given me this Gray House to shelter and keep me while he is away. I shall have enough to stay busy while Hiram chases the leviathan across the globe. Perhaps he shall also leave me with child. He has come to me these many nights since our wedding. Should I bear Hiram's child, my joy should be complete.*

Mary, Mary. Kelly shook her head and stood, heading for the bathroom window. Thinking that a child would preserve a marriage, would halt any abuse. Her own mother had thought the same, once. It hadn't helped any of them. Funny, she hadn't thought of her mother in a year or more. What woman would surrender her own child to the state and not fight for her? She'd died in a drunken stupor when Kelly was twelve, one week after Kelly had moved in with Lottie and Chuck.

Part of her wondered if Mary Gray ever found the peace she sought with having a child. Sleep had overcome Kelly, and she told herself the answers for the quilt weren't inside Mary's journal.

Kelly leaned on the windowsill. This window had a view of the gardens, still coming into bloom. The lush green lawn was thicker than when she'd first paid a visit to Gray House. There was Tom, pouring something at the base of the rosebushes from a box. Then he reached with his strong hands to pour from a watering can.

A tough guy, a gardener. Tom straightened, then glanced around the yard. He looked at a blooming rosebush, then leaned in to sniff. The gentle gesture made her chuckle. How a man acted when he thought no one was looking said a lot about him.

There were men like Peyton Greaves, who kept up quite an appearance and fooled a lot of people. Probably still fooled some people, even though Kelly had resisted the temptation to drag his name publicly through the hog pen and see how he liked mud sticking to his name.

Then there were men like Jenks, who didn't care what anyone thought. But he couldn't hurt her anymore, nor any child under his roof.

But Tom Pereira . . . he made her feel safe, after only a few encounters. Quite a contrast from that first day when she saw his face in the window. She moved from her spot at the window before he saw her face in the glass. As she did so, she saw Tom grab his head and sink to the grass.

Kelly shoved all thoughts of the quilt aside and ran, her feet skidding on the parquet floor. She pounded down the stairs, whirling around the balustrade and down the hall toward the kitchen. Blasting the back door open with a bang, Kelly stumbled on the back steps but caught her balance as she ran for Tom.

Tom lay prostrate on the ground, his arms at his sides, his body clenching as if in an enormous spasm. Kelly fell to her knees at his side. What was the thing to do when someone had a seizure? Lottie once had a foster child with epilepsy. They'd been told to let Jana alone, but make sure she couldn't hurt herself on anything.

"Hang on, Tom." She pulled out her phone and called 911. After speaking with the dispatcher, Kelly set the phone to the side while the phone line was live. A few more seconds, and Tom fell limp.

Kelly allowed herself to touch his forehead. "Tom, I called an ambulance. It'll be here soon. I hope you're not mad at me for calling someone." The faint wail of a siren emerged from the sounds of the city.

"Shouldn't have called," he mumbled. "I'm fine . . ."

"No, collapsing into a seizure in the backyard is not fine." She studied his face. His eyes were closed, his forehead wet with perspiration. She reached for his cheek, clammy to her touch.

The siren's wail bit into the air as it intensified, the ambulance rolling to a halt in the driveway. Kelly stood as the first EMT left the vehicle.

"He started having a seizure." She gestured to Tom's form on the grass. "He stopped about a minute or so ago. He said something to me, but he's out again."

The EMTs moved past her, one of them pushing a gurney. The tallest male looked at her and asked, "Do you know anything about his medical history?"

She shook her head. "I really don't know. I've only just met him, really."

The shorter EMT reached for Tom's wrist. "He's got a medic alert bracelet. Tom Pereira, age thirty-one. Seizures and TBI."

"TBI?" Kelly asked, but not really expecting an answer from them as they checked vital signs and radioed information to the hospital.

The tall one looked up at her somberly. "Traumatic brain injury."

"We're bringing him in." The young one stood.

"Which hospital?" She knew she couldn't go with him, but at least she could follow and he could wake up to a familiar face. Also, if he had family, maybe she could reach them.

"New Bedford General."

Tom opened his eyes to see an ambulance ceiling. The engine roared, siren blared, and the gurney shook. "Take me back."

"Mr. Pereira, we're almost to the hospital," said a trim young man who looked barely out of high school. A high wind could snap him like a twig.

"I don't want to go. I'll be fine. Just need to sleep it off. This has happened before." Honestly, Kelly should have listened to him. He knew he'd babbled something to her before he zoned out. He did remember how soft her hand was as she touched his cheek. Of course, she'd worried. He hadn't told her anything about his history. Didn't think he needed to. Maybe that had been a mistake.

But if his neurologist heard about this . . . Tom tried to sit up.

"Oh no you don't." Twig-boy pushed him down with a capable wiry hand. The kid had strength. "You're going to get checked out before they send you home."

"Great." He knew he was making a tough patient, but he couldn't help himself.

"Do you have a headache, Mr. Pereira?"

"A little."

"Intensity level on a scale of one to ten, one being almost none and ten being the worst pain you've ever felt?"

"Uh, maybe a six." His head pounded a little, but he could handle it. He hadn't had a headache in several months.

"Okay." As the EMT made a note, the radio squawked.

Tom forced himself to close his eyes and let the sway of the ambulance lull him back into the quiet. As long as Kelly didn't figure out a way to contact his family, he'd deal with the hospital visit just fine.

Kelly paced the emergency room lobby. They wouldn't let her back with Tom. She got that. She kept glancing up every time the glass double doors whooshed open to see if Mrs. Pereira had arrived.

The older woman sounded concerned when Kelly called her, thanks to Mrs. Acres giving her an emergency contact number. Surely, this constituted an emergency. Mrs. Pereira had said she would come right away.

The doors opened again, and in came an older woman with hair as fiercely curly as Tom's, with a nose like his, and warm, brown eyes. Mrs. Pereira, of course.

"Mrs. Pereira." Kelly approached the woman who wore a simple pantsuit and slip-on loafers. She suddenly remembered her own appearance, wearing her favorite ancient jeans and button-down work shirt, covered with equally ancient stains.

"You must be Kelly." The woman embraced her, which came as a surprise. "Thank you for calling me. That boy of mine won't. Stubborn."

"Well, I'm not surprised." Kelly shook her head. "I mean, we barely know each other, Tom and I. But he seems like he could be stubborn."

"You have that part of him figured out, though."

"Do you want a coffee or anything? Or a soda?" Kelly gestured to a bank of vending machines on one wall. "We might be here a while. Of course, they won't tell me anything, since I'm not family."

"I'm fine right now." Mrs. Pereira squared her shoulders. "As far as not knowing anything, I'll see what I can do."

Kelly nodded and watched the older woman go to the reception desk before she headed to the vending machine for a cold drink. She purchased a soda then found a pair of cushioned chairs in a quiet corner.

Mrs. Pereira joined her shortly. "Well, they wouldn't tell me anything, either. But they did say they would let Tom know I'm here." She sank onto the chair beside Kelly.

"That's good. I'm not sure if they told him I was there . . ." Kelly took a sip of her drink. "So what happened to Tom, that he has these seizures, if you don't mind me asking?"

"It happened during his military service. A freak accident, nothing combat related." Mrs. Pereira frowned. "Anyway, he's done great for a long time. I hadn't thought about it in a long time, either. I finally felt like we had a break, that Tom was going to have a break, too. So how do you two know each other again?"

"I . . . I just started working at Gray House. I'm a textile conservator and they hired me to restore an old quilt. So I'm living and working on-site."

"Are you from around here?"

"I'm . . . I'm from the Haverhill area. I was able to break my lease and move here."

"What does your family think about you moving just like that?"

"I . . . um . . . I really don't have any family to speak of." Kelly hadn't admitted that to anyone since, well, she couldn't remember.

"Everyone has family, dear. I can't imagine you not having anyone to care about where you are."

"There's Lottie, my last foster mother, and her husband, Chuck. I fostered out of their care after I graduated high school, but I kept in touch with her." She should have called Lottie again, she realized, since her arrival in New Bedford.

"Ah, I see." Mrs. Pereira patted her hand. "If you ever need anything, call me."

"Thanks. I appreciate that."

They fell into silence, but it didn't feel as if she waited with a stranger. The sensation was a nice one. An open invitation to call the woman. Well, she wouldn't if she didn't have to. One lesson learned over the years: counting on people didn't work very well. She had her own motto of sorts. If it was just her and God, she'd manage okay because He was watching out for her.

The buzz of the waiting room surrounded them, and Kelly watched Mrs. Pereira's chin sink lower toward her chest. She settled back on her own chair. She could leave now, knowing that Tom had a ride home once he was through. She could check on the quilt and see if it was dry yet. It probably was. But if Mrs. Pereira woke, Kelly didn't want to leave her alone.

At last Tom emerged from behind one of the large double doors that led back to the treatment rooms. Kelly sat up straight and gently tapped Mrs. Pereira's arm. "Tom's done."

He scanned the room, then caught sight of them and nodded. "I'm fine. They wanted to do an MRI, but I said no."

"Oh, Tommy . . . ," Mrs. Pereira said as she rose. "Couldn't you have waited?"

"No, I'm feeling better now, and they told me I need to see my VA doc. So I will." He gave his mother a hug. "You didn't need to come. How'd you know?" He released his mother and shot a look at Kelly.

"Uh, Mrs. Acres," Kelly said. "She gave me your emergency contact information. I . . . I hope you didn't mind."

Tom paused. He glanced from his mother, to Kelly, then back to his mother again. "No. And thanks."

"So, you'll both come for supper tonight?" Mrs. Pereira looked at both of them.

"Well, I . . . ," Kelly began.

"I don't know . . . ," Tom said.

"Kelly is new in town. The least we can do is show her some kindness, especially since she took such good care of you today. Imagine if you'd been alone." Mrs. Pereira looped her arm through her son's, then tugged Kelly closer with her other hand.

"It wasn't anything, really," Kelly said.

"But it was." Mrs. Pereira nodded.

"Ma, don't worry about it. Kelly's pretty busy . . ."

"Humor me. Your niece and nephew are at the house. They're staying for a couple of days of spoiling." Mrs. Pereira plucked Tom's arm. "We might have a dominoes tournament, playing to one hundred. Winner does dishes."

"All right, I'll be there." Tom smiled. "She's pretty insistent." He glanced at Kelly.

"You're still coming for supper, young lady." Mrs. Pereira nodded.

"All right, then. I . . . I'll see you tonight."

# 7

Tom kept quiet all the way back to Gray House, and thankfully Kelly respected his silence. She'd retreated into her own thoughts as well, it seemed.

He glanced down at the discharge papers on his lap. No driving until seen by his neurologist. Did that mean no motorcycle, either? Technically riding a motorcycle wasn't driving. The ER doc hadn't seen the humor in his challenge, though.

Maybe Kelly coming for supper wasn't a bad idea. They would focus on her instead of asking him the same questions here and there. He could minimize the focus on his seizure today.

He thought ahead to the follow-up visit with the neurologist. It was bad enough that the ER doctor had said no driving until his appointment in a week. He only hoped the neurologist didn't bar him from driving for a longer period of time. Of course, he understood the need for safety and all that. He didn't want to endanger anyone because of his stubbornness.

Kelly pulled into the driveway at Gray House and turned off the engine. She opened her mouth, then closed it. Then she said, "Your mother is very sweet."

He nodded. "She's the best. She really is."

"I'm sorry if I overstepped today, but I didn't know . . ."

"Of course you didn't, and that's okay." The faint traces of a headache pricked his temples. "I guess you should know about the seizures. Did my mother tell you anything?"

"Just that you'd had an injury while in the military."

He sighed and looked across at the lawn, the rosebushes, and the knocked-over box of rose food where he'd collapsed earlier. "Yes, it was an accident. I had a hematoma on my brain after a fall from the back of a tall truck. That plus some fractures in my back gave me a medical discharge from the Army. I've been home about a year now, trying to get life figured out. I . . . I'm a Christian, but sometimes God feels pretty far away."

He watched her nod slowly. Now that he'd spilled as much as he was going to for now, he'd let that bit of info sit with her.

"I'm sorry" was all she could manage at first. "I know how it feels, trying to get life figured out. I'm a Christian, too. One thing I've learned is that in the end, God is all I have."

It was his turn to nod. "This is why I can't go backwards. I'm getting things figured out, little by little. My pastor said something about me getting used to my new reality. This isn't what I was looking for. I wanted to make a career out of serving my country."

"I know what you mean. I never thought I'd end up here." She exhaled sharply, her breath fluffing the ends of her hair that had escaped her ponytail and dangled as wisps in front of her eyes.

"Guess we'd better get back to work."

"I guess so." She looked at him and blinked. "I figure it won't do much good to tell you to be careful."

He gave her a rueful grin. "Probably not. But I'll pace myself as long as you don't call my mother again."

"Deal," she said, opening the driver's side door. "Besides, I have too much to do this afternoon."

He snapped to attention at her remark, then realized she was joking as she grinned at him.

---

Kelly sauntered into the house, flying on her little wave of orneriness. He was getting to her, and she needed to make herself quit. She refused to listen to that *something* she felt was calling out inside her when Tom admitted his life wasn't going the direction he'd intended, through circumstances beyond his control. She always liked cheering for the underdog, the fighter, the one who looked at the world like they had something to prove.

Because the world could be cruel. So, so cruel. She carried her purse and keys up to the room she called hers. The house was massive and she didn't feel comfortable leaving her purse and keys casually on the countertop or in the front hallway.

She glimpsed Mary Gray's journal on the chest of drawers. Much as she'd love to sit for a while and puzzle out some of Mary's fine script, she should return her attention to the quilt. Kelly entered the hallway and headed for the bathroom once belonging to Captain Gray.

The quilt lay where she left it, on its layer of towels. She touched the delicate fibers. Still damp. Perhaps she'd better transfer it to another set of towels. She laid another rectangle of dry towels on the floor, then tiptoed around the edge of the quilt. Lifting the corners slowly, she folded the cloth over itself in half, then half again. The backing had been white, or at least a shade of ecru. The burn marks showed up on this side of the quilt as well.

She laid the folded quilt on the layer of fresh towels, then kicked the soggy towels out of the way. Then she knelt beside the quilt and felt the folded layers again. She unfolded the quilt and ran her fingers across the surface.

This was it for the day. The poor quilt had seen enough trauma after being cast off for so long. Tomorrow the real work began. She needed to set up a workroom, likely in the drawing room downstairs.

Kelly left the quilt drying in the semi-darkened room and went to check her e-mail. Lottie had written, and Kelly's conscience pinged her. She still hadn't called Lottie back.

*Dear Kelly,*

*I hope you arrived safely in New Bedford. If you need anything, let me know. Sewing supplies, anything. I know that you have traveled for your work before, but this feels different. Please call when you can. I hope to hear from you soon.*

*Love,*
*Lottie*

*P.S. Someone called yesterday, asking about your mother. I thought that was extremely odd.*

So did she. Kelly bit her lip. Who would be asking about Frances Simmons Frost, dead and gone for sixteen years?

Kelly picked up her phone and called Lottie, who answered after the second ring.

"Kelly!"

"Hi, I got your message yesterday, and your e-mail. I'm sorry I haven't called."

"Not to worry. I knew you would. So, tell me about the house. I bet it looks like a museum."

"It does, sort of. One that hasn't been taken care of for quite some time. I'm sure back in the day it was the best in New Bedford. Right now, it needs some TLC."

"Maybe this will be the first of more jobs for you."

"Now that would be amazing," Kelly said. "Not to change the subject, but you said someone called, asking about my mother?"

"Yes. It was the strangest thing. I told them you'd been part of our family since you were twelve, and before that I wasn't sure where you lived."

Kelly shivered. "I don't like the idea of someone hunting for information about me or my family. Such as it is. Or was."

"Well, they didn't say who they were, and I didn't give them any more information than that."

"Did they ask where I am now?"

"No, they didn't. And don't you worry. I won't tell them where you are."

"Thank you." She almost brought up the issue of Peyton and the Boston Fine Arts Museum, but Lottie would know she was leaving out part of the whole painful story.

"Are you doing okay, dear?"

"Yes, I am. It's good to hear from you."

"I'm praying for you, Kelly. You find yourself a good church while you're away."

"Thanks. I'll . . . I'll try."

They ended the call and Kelly set her phone down on the chest of drawers next to Mary Gray's journal. Lottie knew her better than anyone. *Find yourself a good church*. Easier said than done, at least for her. And she'd told Lottie she would try. As far as the prayers were concerned, Kelly welcomed them.

Before the fidgets set in, Kelly decided to walk the house and clear a space in the drawing room to make a workshop. She'd told Mr. Chandler and Firstborn Holdings that she needed certain supplies that she couldn't bring from Haverhill. They'd arrived and were tucked into a corner of the butler's pantry, along with four six-foot folding tables.

She descended the stairs and entered the front sitting room that overlooked County Street. Too much light, not enough control over the ultraviolet rays that came through the glass, even covered with inner shutters. Exposure over time would harm the delicate fabric—not that it could be injured much more.

She moved past the dining room where she'd laid the quilt on the table that first day, and pulled open yet another set of wooden pocket doors. The opening doors echoed off an expanse of wooden floor. A ballroom. Not large by her imagination, but large enough for a dozen couples to make their way around the room, with a small platform in the corner for musicians.

The fireplace had to be marble, coal black with creamy white striations and veins running through it. Kelly had visited the mansions of Newport, Rhode Island, as an undergraduate student. This fireplace wasn't nearly as grand, but for its time and for New Bedford, it was colossal.

Heavy curtains framed floor-to-ceiling windows. Kelly tugged on the thick fabric of one pair, and pulled the edges together. The level of light in the room decreased. She could work in this room just fine. The windows looked out on the side gardens, green with new growth, thanks to Tom's hard work.

She resisted the urge to check up on him. He was a grown man. Yet, a grown man who'd suffered a head injury and had just had a seizure that morning. She squinted out the window to see if Tom was working among the rows of plants and shrubs, or in the greenhouse.

Kelly pried herself away from the windowpane, pulled the curtains back into place, and slipped the tiebacks around them. She already knew the main floor contained the kitchen, a parlor, a drawing room, a music room, a dining room, and a ballroom. The second floor held four bedrooms, two bathrooms, and a study. She'd already seen the third floor with its servants' quarters, and the lookout room that capped off the space of the house.

She ambled to the kitchen and pulled out the takeout leftovers. There went Tom, heading from the greenhouse and in the direction of the back door to Gray House.

He rapped on the door before he opened it. "I thought I'd get some water. It's a little warm in that greenhouse."

"Sure. I'll get you a glass."

"I can do it. Just point me in the direction of the right cabinet."

"Bottom shelf, by the sink." Kelly nodded toward the cabinet. "There's ice in the freezer, bottled water in the fridge."

His movements were smooth as he crossed the kitchen, denying any evidence of the seizure. She didn't ask him how he felt because she already knew the answer.

"The gardens look good."

Tom nodded. "There was a ton of overgrowth. I had to prune, a lot. It looks pretty decent now, but next year it'll be back to its prior glory."

"You sound like you'll probably be around here by then."

He pulled a bottle of water out of the refrigerator and poured some into the glass, then plunked in a trio of ice cubes. "Maybe, maybe not."

"The inside of this place is amazing. Some dust and polish, some TLC to the textiles, and it'll be a showpiece again. I found a ballroom, and that's where I'll set up a workshop for the quilt." She hesitated a moment. Tom glanced at her. "I also found Mary Gray's journal."

"Mary Gray?"

"Captain Hiram Gray's wife. He's the one who built this house."

Tom nodded. "I've heard stories about him. He actually went to seminary, then left the preacher-hood, so to speak, and went to the ocean instead."

"Huh." Kelly thought for a moment. "A pretty righteous man, then. I started reading Mary's journal. I've read at least one section where he hit her for speaking out of turn. But what else do you know about this place?"

"It was owned by the Grays until a fire sometime in the 1800s." He took a swallow of water. "Now Firstborn Holdings owns it."

"Too bad it didn't stay in the family."

"It happens to a lot of old places like this." Tom shrugged. "Some families couldn't keep up with the lifestyle after the whale oil industry died, so unless there was another money-maker, the property would change hands and leave the family."

Kelly nodded. "That's sad."

"That's how it goes." He paused for a moment. "Look, if you don't really want to go to my family's for supper tonight, that's okay."

"You sound like you don't want me there."

"I, uh . . ." His ears turned red. "No, it's not that. My mother comes on a little strong."

"You should thank God every day that you have a mother who loves you like that." Kelly cleared her throat. "I need to check on something upstairs. Holler at me when you're ready to go for supper and I'll be ready."

She left before he could say more. Tom Pereira was a blessed man. Maybe he knew it, maybe his mother's concern bugged him a little. But for some reason, seeing Tom's mother had reawakened the old ache. Frances Frost had taken her issues with her to the grave, but Kelly still wrestled with them sometimes, like now.

She scaled the stairs and entered her room, the lady's room, and picked up Mary Gray's journal once again. Maybe she could read some more about Gray House itself. Tom mentioned a fire at one point. She recalled the scent of smoke in the little boy's closet. Could smoke smell linger that long?

Kelly situated herself in the side chair close to the window and opened the journal.

*December 1850*

*I cradle an infant, much as Mary did in Bethlehem that first Christmas morn. What thoughts she must have had, looking upon the Savior, nestled in a manger. I share his mother's name, but my child sleeps in a handcrafted cradle, made by one of the carpenters in town. My son. Nay, our son, Hiram, bears his father's name. Only one letter since Hiram's departure in March. I wrote him as soon as I thought it safe, while carrying a child. One must be careful in such matters, my mother told me once. Little Hiram shall likely be walking by the time his father returns.*

So Mary had her longed-for child. Kelly smiled. The woman sounded contented. Maybe Mary had a happy ending after all, or at least a measure of peace while her husband was thousands of miles away, hunting whales.

Kelly read a few more entries, speaking of the baby's growth, the long winter, and how Mary longed to hear from the captain.

*January 1851*

*I have started another quilt, the Mariner's Compass. It is more difficult than most patterns, but its symbol gives me hope. The Lord directs our steps, the Master over the course through our sea of life. We look to His Word as our compass. Hiram would most definitely approve of this theme. I fear my sewing skills are not up to the challenge, but my seamstress Leonora will help fix any of my shortcomings. Leonora is a Godsend, the sister of the carpenter who built little Hiram's cradle. I am thankful for God's providence.*

Kelly had to smile at Mary's upbeat attitude. Having an upbeat attitude was easy when it seemed all was going your way. But what thrilled her most of all was reading the reference to the quilt. The idea of touching fabric that Mary had touched, well over a century before, gave her goose bumps.

*February 1851*

*One year, and Hiram has been gone. I can see him in our young one's face, with the furrowed brow and loud cries. He seems to have been born with the same sense of right and wrong. How a child knows such deep things is a mystery to me. From his nursery chair, he seems to scold me with his infant's glare.*

*Esteban Delgado, a local craftsman, built a beautiful infant's bed for him, from timbers from an old ship. He is a good man from a humble family. He inquired last week about young Hiram and his solid bed. I told him that Hiram thrived and rested well.*

*Before he left, he made one more inquiry. "My English is not so good, I know. But I wish to learn to read. Will you teach me?"*

*I could not say no to his dark eyes.*

# 8

The old man was having a good day and was seated by the window that looked out onto a busy street. The late afternoon traffic zoomed along, snaking north to south, south to north along the coast.

"So, so busy we all are," the old man said as he entered the room. "Here today, gone tomorrow, life is but a vapor."

He loosened his tie and plunked himself down on the spare chair beside the bed. "Did you have everything you need?"

"I need nothing but to know that the past is set right."

He tried not to roll his eyes. Gestures like that were only fitting for an unruly, disrespectful teenager. And he had always respected the old man. Why not? He'd given him everything, from youth on up.

"It's not your job to set the past right," he said as gently as he could. "Some things just . . . are. I have a feeling that the universe makes it so. We all get what we deserve in the end."

The old man waved off his words. "Not always . . . not always. I don't have much time left, and I'm going to do what I can to upset the apple cart."

Now *this* wasn't what he expected. "Don't do anything rash. Are you sure you're feeling all right?"

"Better than I have in weeks. You're my lawyer, so don't give me any grief over what I'm going to ask you to do."

The old man's next words made his hands turn into fists. Delirious and unstable. He should call the old man's doctor right away.

———⊗⊗⊗———

"So, what do you know about your family tree?" Dave Winthrop asked at the conclusion of their brief meeting. They'd already walked the inside of the townhouse, and Tom made his measurements. He'd get the permits and do the best he could on this job.

The dining room contained, as Tom had expected, a framed parchment outlining the Winthrop family tree for several centuries. The family tree looked strong, generations stretching back.

"I don't know much, just that we've been here in New Bedford for a long, long time," Tom said. "We had some ship-builders and seamen in our ranks, a few factory workers. Blue collar people. That's about all I know."

"Sometimes it helps a man to know where he comes from, Tom." Dave clapped him on the back. "You strike me as the kind of man who could use a little direction."

"How do you know about me? We've only met once."

"I always check up on people I hire," said Dave. "You're from good stock, better than you might imagine. There's no shame in hard work, and I think you know that. Plus, you served your country."

"Yes, I was in the military." What was the guy getting at?

"I was West Point, class of '72. Spent thirty years in the Army, retired. Worked civil service for a while until I decided there was plenty of life left to live and not behind a desk, so I retired again."

Tom nodded. "You got your years in. The problem is, I didn't. I'm not college material. So all I have are these." He held up his hands.

"As long as you keep that in mind, you'll do well. Don't give up on the idea of your education, though."

"Thanks for the advice." Tom closed his notepad. Mom would keep supper waiting for him and Kelly, who waited outside in her car. She'd been stubborn enough not to let him drive his motorcycle to the house and he figured he wouldn't fight her about it.

"I can see you have places to go, things to do, and people waiting for you, like the pretty lady in the car outside." Dave shook hands with him. "But take a look back on your tree, then look ahead. You might be surprised at what you find."

"Thanks for the advice. I'll get you an estimate and call you tomorrow."

"That sounds like a plan." Dave nodded.

Tom joined Kelly outside, and off they want to his parents' house. Maybe it wouldn't turn out so bad after all. Tonight she'd be everyone's focus instead of him. That could be a problem, especially if his family chose to link them romantically. However, maybe his health wouldn't be their main subject of conversation tonight.

He gave her a sideways glance and let it linger. Of course, she was beautiful. Not the model, knock-you-over looker type. But more of the once you starting looking at her, you didn't want to stop type. Proportioned nose, full lips, yet not pouty—why some younger women persisted in taking "duck face" photos of themselves was beyond his understanding—and her eyes . . .

She met his gaze. "Are you feeling okay? Did I make a wrong turn? I'm sure you'd speak up and make some crack about women drivers if I did." She grinned, then snapped her attention back to the road.

"I'm . . . I'm fine." He cleared his throat. "I know I mentioned bracing yourself for my family. They might start to think we're, uh, a couple or something."

"Well, I thought about that, too."

"My family's reaction or us being a couple?" He couldn't resist teasing her.

"Uh . . ." Her face flushed red. "I'm going to let them know I've only moved here for the summer and you and I have only just met. Of course, your mother had a hand in supper tonight, both literally and figuratively. I'm willing to guess she's probably playing matchmaker."

He released his breath. "Good. We'll just go with the flow, then."

"That's fine with me."

---

Tom might as well not have been there tonight, as much as Kelly was peppered with questions about her family, her career, how she'd gotten the job here. She stammered a bit when admitting her foster child background, but her face glowed when speaking of Lottie and Chuck, the couple she considered parents. Chuck had passed away two years ago after years of heart trouble. When she said the words, a shadow flickered across her face.

Meanwhile, Tom's own father scarcely said five words to him during the meal. What was it with his dad? What would be enough for him to say, "Son, you did good. Life dealt you a poor hand, but with God's help, you've made it through."

Maybe because Tom wasn't satisfied with only making it through. Not when his own brother had far excelled him. But if anything were to happen to Pop . . . The idea made him grip his fork a little tighter.

"So, Kelly, you're working on a quilt, did you say?" his mother asked.

"Yes. I don't get too many of those to work on, actually. I'll definitely have the chance to brush up on my fine needlework. I've been instructed to find matching fabric and repair all the holes in the quilt blocks, but I'm afraid it's not quite that simple."

"Why's that?"

"The newer fabric and stitches are strong, which ends up making the older needlework more vulnerable." Kelly swept a strand of hair over one ear. "If you want something to break, you want it to be at the newer stitching, not do further damage to the old. Which is why sometimes trying to restore something only hastens its deterioration."

"Well, Miss Frost," Tom's father spoke up. "I'm glad you were there for my son. He's a bit stubborn, don't know where he gets that from. But supper doesn't seem to be thank-you enough."

"This is fine, Mr. Pereira. It's nice to be able to sit among a family tonight." She grinned that smile of hers at them. Tom hadn't paid enough attention to it now, but it almost had that Julia Roberts megawatt quality to it. He yanked his focus back to his nephew, who was tugging at his elbow. Hopefully, his father would quit pointing out Tom's "issues," as he liked to call them.

"What's going on, Hunter?" He asked his nephew.

"You plant gardens, right?"

"I'm learning."

"My mom's plant that I gave her for Mother's Day is dying," Hunter said, his face drooping.

"What kind of plant are we talking here?"

"It's an anwall."

"Anwall?"

"I mean annual." His nephew's face reddened.

"Annuals only live one season, buddy."

"You should see my garden," Mom called from two seats down. "It's growing like crazy. Maybe you and Kelly can go take a look at it while we get the dishes in the dishwasher and coffee brewing. Got some fresh Dunkin at the store."

Tom looked down at his empty plate. It was a setup, for sure. So long as Kelly understood that, they should both be fine. "I guess I'm ready if you are."

Kelly nodded. "I'll take our plates to the kitchen." As he followed her into the kitchen, she whispered over her shoulder, "Might as well get this over with."

The dishes left for the others to fight over, Tom led Kelly out the back door. "And now, for the garden." He held the door open and gestured for her to pass.

"For the garden," she said in mock low tones.

The twilight air outside held a fair amount of humidity. Maybe there'd be more rain in the forecast. Tom hadn't noticed the forecast, and he ought to. Much as he'd joked about gardening, he knew that the powers that be over Gray House took the garden very seriously. As did he, he realized.

His parents had tilled up a large section of ground, taking up the corner where he and his brother had once knocked a baseball around and passed the football back and forth. Change had come to the family home.

"It's nice out here," Kelly said.

"You mean the quiet is nice," Tom countered. "I have only one niece and nephew, but when they're spending time with Mom and Pop, their noise multiplies."

"You don't mind it one bit, though, do you?"

"Nah. They're great kids. It seems like they were just born, and now Hunter is getting closer to the top of my shoulder every time I see him." Tom eyed the first row of plants, shooting tall like his brother's children. His parents' tomato plants were thriving, with little green misshaped spheres promising plenty of red fruit in the next few weeks.

"I had lots of brothers and sisters growing up, sort of." Kelly bent over to inspect the radishes, still petite. "The ones I count, probably twelve altogether."

"Do you keep in touch with any of them?" He couldn't help but ask.

"Only through Lottie. I get pretty busy with my job . . ." Her voice drifted off. "They've done the same. Some of them ended up doing pretty well for themselves, others not so well. Some we don't hear from at all."

"Ah." He inspected a row of lettuce.

"Your parents are neat." Kelly stood up straight and faced him, then eyed the house behind them. "It must've been great to grow up here. Your parents' home just . . . just oozes love."

"Yeah. They've been good parents."

"And your dad, I know he must be so proud of you."

"Proud of me? For what?" The words came out more sharply than he'd meant.

"You're not a quitter, in spite of everything you've been through." Kelly's chin lifted a fraction of an inch. "You could have given up, not even attempted to have a life, played the woe-is-me card. But here you are."

"A glorified gardener. Ha." He shoved his hands into his pockets and continued along the garden path.

Kelly trotted along beside him. "That's better than a lot of things you could have been. One of my former 'brothers' is serving a life sentence in prison because of a stupid bar fight. Another one of my former foster sisters is, well, we don't know

**85**

how or where she is. Lottie ended up taking care of her children, both born with classic symptoms of being exposed to crack before birth. I could go on, but I won't."

"Tell that to my father. Did you hear him in there? Talking about me as if I were a child."

"You're still his son. He probably sees you that way. I bet you were the one always getting your knees skinned."

Her humor cooled his aggravation just a few degrees, as long shadows from the house devoured the remaining patches of light in the backyard. "Ha." He bit back any number of things he could say to her, none of which would help anything. "I'm still just a gardener."

"Goodness, Eeyore. Maybe I'll take back what I said about the woe-is-me attitude. Don't you remember where we were earlier? A man wants to pay you to install flooring and tile in his beautiful but likely outdated townhouse." She poked his arm.

He caught her hand in his, and he allowed himself to brush back some of those wispy strands of hair from her cheek, the same strands that had kept drifting into her way at supper. "You're sweet, Kelly Frost. And funny. I like that."

"Thanks . . ."

The back door banged. Tom released Kelly's hand and turned toward the house.

Hunter pounded down the back steps, off the deck, and approached them at a full run. "Uncle Tom! Did you see the squash?"

---

Kelly wrangled the six-foot table into the center of the ballroom and slid it next to the matching table. This would give her at least a hard surface to support the quilt as she worked on repairs. Nothing would restore it to its former glory, but she would strive to keep Firstborn Holdings happy. Of course, Mr. William Chandler hadn't returned her call for a request for more information.

Her phone buzzed atop the marble mantel, so she trotted off to answer. Mr. Chandler. Finally. "This is Kelly Frost."

"Ms. Frost, I received your message. Is there an issue with the quilt?"

"Not exactly. I'm a bit hesitant, however, to use this new fabric on the blocks. I'm making some templates of the pattern so I can cut—"

"I really don't need an explanation. Just continue on the project. That's what you're being paid for."

In times past, Kelly would have slung her phone against the wall. That was the impulsiveness of youth. She thought better of it now. "I understand. I'm going to complete this project to the best of my ability, but often I find that clients have unrealistic expectations of the results."

"Keep me apprised of your progress. Have a nice day, Ms. Frost."

"You too, thank you." She was talking to a broken connection. "That figures," she said to the silent phone.

Ever since the disaster with Peyton and the Boston Fine Arts Museum, she found herself doubting her skill. She pulled on a clean pair of acid-free work gloves, then removed the quilt from the acid-free cardboard box where she'd stored it once it was dry.

She spread out the quilt on the tables until the center Mariner's Compass lay directly in the midpoint of the tables. Shades of blue, brown, green, and gray made up the points of all five compasses. Shades of the sea made up the quilt on what was once a stark-white background.

The task at hand kept thoughts of Tom from the forefront of her mind. Never mind that she'd tried to sleep last night, but remembering his gentle touch on her hand and her hair kept her awake. It was what she and her girlfriends back in college would have called a "kissable moment."

The moment had fled, thankfully, when the nephew had popped into the backyard. Not that part of her wouldn't welcome a kiss. But it was too soon for her. She wasn't given to a casual smooch here and there. Peyton had been her first big deal, and look what that had gotten her.

"Lord, I need your help with this one," she said aloud in the large room, her voice echoing off the walls. She'd returned to her faith after her crash and burn with Peyton, after she'd sunk lower than she could have imagined. Relearning to pray easily had been like learning a new language.

"This place is not my home, Lord, and I don't see myself being here much past late summer. I know Tom has issues; I have issues. Please guide our steps." Her thoughts swirled as she stared at the quilt. God wasn't the author of confusion, and she was letting her thoughts yank her emotions around. *Breathe, Kelly. Breathe.*

Nothing had happened last night, and she still had a job to do. *Peace, peace.*

She took out her template material and studied the center compass of the quilt, its points stretching like rays of the sun from the middle of the pattern. A challenging bit of needle-work, even for an expert.

Mary had had an even hand with the quilt. Or maybe it was her helper, Leonora. Tiny stitches accented the pattern of each compass ray. A number were gone, but the ones that remained spoke of the care Mary had taken when stitching her project.

Maybe she ought to follow Mary's lead and see if Willa was interested in some freelance work. She picked up her phone and dialed.

"Willa, it's Kelly Frost."

"Hey, there. How's New Bedford treating you?"

"I have a *lot* of work to do, is how it's treating me."

"I was going to call you, but I'm actually in Newport."

If Willa was in Newport, that probably meant . . . "Ah, I see."

"I'm working for Jonna." The line went silent, and Kelly looked at the phone to see if the connection was lost. Nope. "Kelly?"

"I'm still here."

"I should have said something to you." Her apologetic tone sounded genuine.

"No, you didn't have to." Kelly almost wanted to warn Willa, but she stopped. Willa had nothing to fear from Jonna, save Willa's skill one day outpacing the more experienced conservator's. "You are working on your career, and I should congratulate you. So, congratulations. I mean it."

"Well, thanks. I'm relieved. I really respect you, Kelly. Maybe we could meet halfway and poke through some shops or something."

"You know, after sitting hunched over a quilt all day, that will probably be ideal." Trust Willa's more youthful energy to drag Kelly away from her work.

"Just let me know, okay?"

"I'll do that." She ended the call and set her phone back down. She'd learned to absorb herself in her work. It was just her and the fibers, as she negotiated some life back into them.

Kelly held up a paper chart she'd made from the quilt pattern. More than one hundred numbered blocks, frayed and damaged, not counting the main surface of the quilt, the binding, plus the backing. If she started now, she might get a third or more of the numbered blocks drawn. She was fashioning new patterns for each damaged block, so each facet of the quilt would have its own custom-made block without putting undue stress on the old.

Already she was congratulating herself. She had too much work to do here to focus on Tom and any weird imaginings. She had a career to rescue, and any diversions could rip that away from her. She wasn't about to give up what she had for a man, not even sweet yet sometimes glum Tom.

Piece by piece, each section took shape. The light in the room changed as the day wore on and the sun passed around the house. As she made her template, she numbered it according to the chart she'd made of the pattern.

Her back ached and her stomach growled. Kelly stood and stretched. One foot had gone numb from her perch on the stool, hunched over the quilt. She limped around the ballroom as her toes tingled back to life again.

Finally, it was good to feel as though she'd made a good start on renewing the pattern. Much, much work lay ahead of her. She touched the fabric of the quilt top. "Hang in there. It'll take a while, but we'll get you there."

# 9

No driving for thirty days until after we get the follow-up MRI results." Dr. Yau wrote something on Tom's chart. "That means no motorcycle, either."

"All right." The words tasted bitter in Tom's mouth. The doctor's orders held no element of shock for him. This had happened before, immediately after his life-changing injury, and the time period had been six months. *Lord, not six months.* Dr. Yau didn't tell him, but Tom knew well enough that if at the end of thirty days the MRI wasn't clear, then it would be another thirty days.

"Schedule your follow-up appointment at the reception desk, and I'll see you in a month." Dr. Yau rose from his chair, and Tom stood as well. Dr. Yau put his hand on Tom's shoulder. "This is just a precaution, you know."

"I do. Thanks." Tom nodded as they left the examining room. His sister-in-law was in the waiting room and stood as he entered. His nephew and niece were busy studying the aquarium at one end of the room.

"So?" she asked. "What did he say?"

"No driving for a month."

"Aw, I'm sorry." She glanced in the direction of the aquarium. "C'mon, guys."

Tom shrugged. "It'll pass. I've got rides. I'll get where I need to go." But nothing compared to the feeling of riding his bike, the air blowing past, the open road beneath him.

He made his follow-up appointment, which wasn't soon enough for him, and joined Angela and the kids outside where they waited in the car. He'd been reduced to being carted around. Sure, it would pass, like he'd just said. He didn't like inconveniencing anyone. Worse, he didn't like not being able to come and go as he pleased.

"Thanks for giving me a ride today," he said as he closed the car door.

"Not a problem, Tom." Angela shifted the car into drive. "We were coming here anyway for the kids' reading program, and the VA Hospital is right on our way."

The kids yammered for almost thirty minutes as they headed back to New Bedford. When Tom caught a pause, he interjected, "You can drop me off at Gray House, on County. I might as well get some work done today."

"Okay." She changed lanes and took the earlier exit instead of the one heading for his mom and pop's place. "House number?"

"Two-forty-eight. It'll be on the right."

She pulled up in front of the house. "Wow, I haven't been to this part of town in forever. I think the last time was when I was in high school, and my history class toured the Rotch-Jones-Duff Mansion down the block."

"Can we go inside?" Hunter said over Tom's shoulder.

"I don't know . . . it's not really ready for visitors." Tom wasn't in the mood to play tour guide.

"But Miss Kelly is there. Will she let us in?" asked Hailey. "I like her."

"She might show you around," Tom replied. "I'll check first. She's been pretty busy working on that old quilt project."

"I'll park on the side street," Angela said as she negotiated the corner. She parked the car. Once Tom pressed the numbers on the key pad to open the side gate, the kids didn't waste time tumbling from the back seat and racing through the side yard.

"I'll beat ya!" Hunter bellowed, his feet pounding the green grass.

Hailey scampered after him.

"If I had half their energy," Angela said as they walked around toward the front door. "I hope we're not a bother to her."

"Like I said, she's busy with the quilt. But I don't think she has any time deadline. I bet she'll be glad to let you at least look through the house."

"I've got to admit, I'm sort of intrigued by the house. I remember even back in high school it was closed up, and that was fifteen years ago." Angela scaled the front steps. Hunter had already grabbed the doorknocker and was packing a wallop on the old wooden door. "Hunter!"

"It's a big house. I want to make sure she can hear us." Hunter frowned.

The front door flew open. Kelly stood there, her blonde hair scraped back into a ponytail. She wore a UMass sweatshirt topping denim capris. She was barefoot, and her toenails were still a shade of perky pink.

"Oh, hi. All of you, hi. Tom, you could have come in the back." She smiled past the kids and at him.

"I wanted to knock on the big door," Hunter said.

"And knock you did." Kelly beamed at the little boy. "I could hear you all the way in the ballroom."

"Ballroom?" asked Hailey. "Like for a Cinderella ball?" Tom tried not to laugh.

"Yes, sort of like a Cinderella ball," Kelly replied.

"Kelly, the kids want to see the inside of the house," Angela said. "Well, me too. Do you mind showing it to us?"

"Oh." Kelly took a few steps back into the entryway. "Come on in, then. I'll give you the grand tour."

Tom hung back as his sister-in-law and her kids entered Gray House. Kelly took them first to the sitting room that overlooked County Street.

"This is probably where the Grays had company when Captain Gray was in town." Kelly stood at the stone fireplace. Hunter and Hailey didn't look impressed. Of course not. There was nothing here to appeal to a child.

He followed along for the tour, never having paid much attention to the inside of the house besides the kitchen. They headed upstairs, the kids leading the way.

"Oh, it's a little boy's room," Hunter said as they entered the first bedroom near the top of the stairs. "Look. Toys." He knelt beside a vintage wooden horse, with a real horsehair mane and wooden wheels.

"Do you know who left them here?" Angela asked.

"I have no idea. Guess I could ask Mrs. Acres at the real estate office about the last family to live here," said Kelly. "Mr. Chandler is a bit hard to reach sometimes." A flicker of aggravation crossed her face. Tom understood that. Chandler was an odd duck.

They continued on through a bathroom with a claw foot bathtub. Feminine and frou-frou room. A few towels hung from an art deco towel bar, and a cloth cosmetics bag was tucked onto one corner of the porcelain sink.

"It must be nice for a woman to have a bathroom all to herself," Angela observed, and both she and Kelly laughed together.

"I'm sure the mother of this house enjoyed it. And this is the room where I'm staying," Kelly announced. "I believe it was originally Mary Gray's bedroom."

The same feminine touches appeared in this room in light blue, with long curtains that lined a pair of windows. She kept everything neat and tidy. A leather-bound book lay on a chest of drawers.

Kelly stopped to pick it up. "My first day moving in, I found this when exploring the house."

"A book?" asked Hailey.

"This is Mary Gray's journal. She wrote about her life a long, long time ago, and she's the one who made the quilt I'm trying to preserve."

"Oh," Angela said, stepping forward, "it's a piece of history. This is priceless, I'm sure, especially tied to the house and the quilt. I certainly don't envy whaling captain's wives. Either they went with their husbands for years on a ship or stayed home alone. I'm not sure which is worse."

"Mary stayed behind, and one of the projects she worked on was this quilt. And she had a baby, too," said Kelly.

"Where did you find that?" Tom heard himself ask.

"I found it inside a bench, up in the lookout room," Kelly said. Then she snapped her fingers. "Oh, I should have told you. The roof up there is leaking, I think. I don't know if you can help with that, but Mr. Chandler never called me back about it."

"A lookout room?" Hunter asked. "You mean like a lookout for ships?"

Kelly nodded. "You can see the harbor from here. I can take you up there. Not much room. It might fit four people, at the most."

Hailey grabbed Kelly's hand. "Take us?"

"Sure. We can all go, take turns looking out the top of the lookout." She led them up another level of stairs, yet another part of the house Tom had never seen. A house of secrets. And the journal Kelly had found.

"Careful, this set of stairs is steeper," Kelly's voice came from above. "And narrower."

The kids scampered up behind her, with Angela following and Tom last of all. He had so much to do, but he'd never been this far inside the house before. They all reached the third floor, which was in stark contrast to the rooms below. Servants' quarters, Tom assumed.

"One more flight of stairs. Much smaller." Kelly smiled at the kids, then her eyes met Tom's. "Let's go see the harbor."

Angela remained below. "It's almost enough to make someone claustrophobic. I'll stay right here."

If anything, Tom needed to see the water damage or leak that Kelly mentioned. "I'm going to take a look. Think there's room for the four of us?"

Kelly nodded. "I think so. Not much. C'mon." She started up the last, narrow wooden staircase. "It's worth the climb."

Once the four of them were inside the lookout room, Tom had to agree. He couldn't stand upright inside the square room, and he could touch opposite windows with both hands at once.

The kids exclaimed about the boats far away. Hailey perched on a low bench and pressed her nose against the glass window "I can see the ocean. I wanna go to the beach."

"Me too." Hunter squinted out at the harbor. "Did someone sleep in this room?"

"I don't think so," Kelly said. "It's kind of small."

"And it's leaky." Tom reached up to the ceiling, inches from the top of his head. "I'll see if I can get a response from Mr. Chandler."

"Good." She looked at him, her eyes filled with concern. "How are you feeling? Did your appointment go well?"

Tom shrugged, and Hailey said, "Uncle Tom can't drive his motorcycle."

"For thirty days," Tom added. "But I'm feeling fine, for the most part."

"I wish I had a spyglass," Hunter said. "Like a sea captain. They could see everything." He held up his hands as if holding an imaginary spyglass.

Tom ran his hands over the ceiling. Part of the wood had a water stain. He didn't relish climbing this high, but he figured the roof would need a quick patch. Or maybe not. It might take a whole lot more work than that.

"Is this all?" Hailey asked. "I want to go downstairs now."

"Go ahead, but go slow. The stairs are steep," said Kelly. She moved to head down the stairs as well, but Tom caught her by the arm.

"Just a second."

She glanced down at his hand on her arm, then up at him. She pulled away. "What is it?"

"Since, uh, I'm not allowed to drive right now, would you pick me up at my apartment in the mornings?"

"Sure, no problem."

"I'd rather not ask my family for rides, and taking the bus would take too long. I can pay you gas money. I'll also need rides to the Winthrop townhouse until I can get one of my buddies to help me."

"Of course. I understand." She blinked at him, and he realized how small the room was at that moment.

"Thanks," he said, before taking the narrow ladderlike stairs to the level below.

They met Angela and the kids at the bottom of the stairs.

"Mom, can we go see the backyard?" Hailey asked. Nobody needed to say that the kids had found some of this tour "boring."

"I can take you outside," Tom said. He knew he'd end up showing the kids the flourishing gardens. His latest instructions from Firstborn Holdings had included locating heirloom rosebushes and rejuvenating the rose garden at Gray House. He'd sat one night at his computer, looking through websites, researching rosebushes. He'd never known there were so many types. Not just red, pink, and yellow roses, but all the names they had.

Hunter and Hailey bounded out of the room into the hallway and were heading down the stairs before he could give them any instructions. He was in for a wild ride.

———

Kelly shut the front door with a sigh. She didn't know how mothers did it. Lottie had been amazing, with as many as six children under her roof at a time. Angie Pereira was amazing, too, corralling her dynamic duo into the back of her car as she waved at Kelly, with a promise to meet up for coffee "sometime."

Tom had ensconced himself in the greenhouse, where Kelly and Angie had met up with him after he showed the children the gardens he was busy restoring. As he talked about the plants and flowers and the garden plans recreated from photos of Gray House, Kelly's curiosity was piqued.

She wanted to find out more about Gray House, remembering her questions when she first moved in. Who else besides

Mary and her Captain Hiram had lived here? When did the house catch on fire? Why the sudden interest in reviving it now? The inside was in decent shape, with most of the furniture and carpets covered in cloths at one time. She didn't envy the early housekeepers in caring for its woodwork, fireplaces, and all its rooms.

Perhaps Mrs. Acres could give her some answers. Over a week since Kelly had moved into the house, and not a peep from the woman.

She headed down the hallway to the ballroom, where the quilt lay on the pair of tables, waiting for her. The vintage fabrics she'd brought with her had been a tricky match to the compass patches. Not all of them would work, so Kelly had to order some vintage cloth. The older, the better. And so she waited. The process was slow, but it needed to be done right.

If Jonna had still been an amiable colleague, Kelly would have asked her if she had anything suitable in her supplies. But Kelly decided to go it alone and not ask for help. It was better that way.

The balmy summer temperatures drew her outside. She decided to venture a walk along County Street toward the real estate office where Mrs. Acres worked. The fresh air would help her, and so would leaving the atmosphere of the house.

Gray House groaned in the wind some days. During the day, it was strange. At night, it made Kelly want to bolt her bedroom door closed, except there was no lock on the door. She shivered. Never afraid of the dark, unless it was an enclosed space where she felt she couldn't breathe.

She locked the front door behind her and ambled to the front iron gate, which she unlocked as well, then relocked once she was on the sidewalk. With its tall stone walls and gated front, Gray House's grounds were almost like a compound that took up half a block. Kelly left the odd feeling behind her and kept along County toward Main Street and Acres and Acres Real Estate.

If Mrs. Acres couldn't give her information, she could always head over a few blocks to the historic district, close to the water. There was some sort of museum and a library, she'd read online. Surely someone knew something about Gray House.

She found the office of Acres and Acres and went inside. The air conditioning was on full blast, sucking the humidity out of the air. Mrs. Acres sprang up from behind her maple desk and met Kelly at the entryway.

"Ms. Frost, how are you? I've been meaning to pop by to make sure you and the house are getting along." Mrs. Acres beamed. Her hair was now a platinum blond. The Maltese lying in a basket in the corner had matching locks.

"I'm doing well, thanks. I think we're getting along fine so far." Kelly rubbed her arms. Goosebumps had popped up as soon as she entered the office. "I've been preparing the quilt and gathering supplies to make repairs."

"Well, I don't envy you a bit." Mrs. Acres shook her head. "Although I've been known to stitch a few baby quilts over time. If you ever need a hand, I'm willing to help."

"Thanks, I appreciate the offer. I'll keep that in mind if I do." The idea of the older woman hovering around the quilt nearly made hives break out among her goose bumps. Kelly didn't plan on needing any help.

"So what brings you here? The pretty weather? Or is there an issue with the house?" Mrs. Acres asked.

"The lookout has a leaky roof on the inside, I've been meaning to let you or Mr. Chandler know."

At the mention of William Chandler, Mrs. Acres stood up straighter, her back stiffening. "Don't call him unless you absolutely must."

"Okay, I did call him, but he hasn't responded."

"That's just as well. I'm glad you came to me about this."

"Well, that's not the only reason I came by. I was wondering if you could tell me anything about the original owners of Gray House." She almost felt silly at the next words she was going to say. "There's a story with the quilt, you know."

"It's part of the historic district," Mrs. Acres moved to a file drawer. "County Street was *the* place to build your home if you were a whaling captain or any of those whale oil industry giants back in the day. They said it was upwind from the smells of the harbor."

"That makes sense to me." Kelly nodded. "But do you have anything that can tell me more about the Grays? When did they sell the home? When did Firstborn Holdings take control of the property?"

"Ah, I see." Mrs. Acres pulled out a file and returned to where Kelly stood. "This is all I have, all that can be shared publicly, that is."

"Okay, thank you."

"Make yourself comfortable over there on the couch." Mrs. Acres gestured to the corner of the office where a leather living room suite waited, complete with coffee table that sported a set of magazines. "Would you like some bottled water?"

"Sure, I'd like that." Kelly carried the file over to the couch and sank onto its buttery softness. The first document in the folder contained an agreement between Acres and Acres for managing the property of Gray House. Nothing new to her here. Mrs. Acres had been managing the property for fifteen years. There were old contracts for lawn care, pouring concrete for the parking slab at the back of the property. But nothing about the Grays, or of Firstborn Holdings.

"Here's your water." Mrs. Acres stood by the arm of the couch. "Have you found anything useful? I'm afraid our records only go back as far as we've been managing the property."

"Thank you." Kelly took a sip from the open plastic bottle. She could see that she'd have to look at the local property records to find some real information. "I don't see anything, really. But maybe you know more than you realize. Did the company ever say why they wanted to hire someone to restore the quilt?"

"No, I can't say as they did. Mr. Chandler is my main contact with Firstborn Holdings. He told me in May, right before I took you to see the quilt," Mrs. Acres replied.

"Out of curiosity, how many others came to Gray House to see the quilt?"

"No one else came. You were the only one."

If she was the only one who came to Gray House to inspect the quilt, that meant she was a sole bidder. She couldn't see how a conservator wouldn't take the time to assess a future project. Why had she been singled out?

—∞∞∞—

The old man was on oxygen now, all the time and not just to sleep at night. He stood at the old man's bedside as he checked his phone.

"I just received a telephone call," he told the old man. "Kelly Frost showed up at the office, asking questions about the house."

"Let her ask." The old man punctuated the statement with a cough. "She is keeping her end of the deal, isn't she?"

"Yes, she is."

"Then that's all I need to know." The old man then commenced with a coughing fit.

"Do I need to call someone?"

The old man raised a wrinkled hand with prominent blue veins. "No. Just let me be."

"All right." He shook his head. He wouldn't say his concern aloud to the old man, but Kelly Frost had better keep her focus on the quilt and leave Gray House alone.

# 10

*June 1851*

My student has accomplished much, as he is a ready learner. I cannot help but feel that what we do is forbidden, even though our time together consists of letters and sounds and words on a page. Esteban is smart and picks up the new words quickly, far more quickly than I would have learned Portuguese.

Somehow I do not miss Hiram's letters. Letters do not come, and my money is running short. I fear for the future at all times, except when Esteban is near. He makes me laugh, and even little Hiram laughs, too. In weaker moments, I imagine that the three of us are a family. I then pray for release from the guilt of such thoughts.

*August 1851*

Esteban claims my thoughts. I can scarcely quilt, scarcely tend to the house, without memories of his eyes, his smile, his voice following me through my day. Such agony. Such sinfulness. It is like a nectar that tastes heavenly as it courses down my throat, yet later on when I think of it, fills my stomach with bile. He has stayed away for nearly a month. I fear that I cannot breathe without him. I pray to God for mercy and forgiveness.

Kelly closed the journal, her cheeks tinged with flames. After a morning's worth of cutting new blocks for the quilt, she decided to give her hands and shoulders a rest. She'd managed to shove the queasiness aside when she kept thinking about Mrs. Acres's revelation, that she was the only bidder for the quilt. Part of her thought she should have asked for more money if she'd known that. Another part felt as if she were under a microscope. Now, reading Mary Gray's journal, she felt as if she were the voyeur, peering into Mary's life.

Looking from the outside in, it wasn't hard to see that Mrs. Hiram Gray was heading down a path that could only end in heartache. Kelly almost spoke a warning to Mary, aloud, as she read the fine script.

But how well she knew the feeling, the giddiness of love. She once imagined a future with Peyton Greaves, even as they walked the corridors of the Boston Fine Arts Museum and stole the kisses of new love behind the statues. Somehow, the chance of them being discovered made the kisses taste sweeter.

Then when she saw the real Mrs. Peyton Greaves one night, Kelly realized she would never bear that name. The woman had been at the spring exhibit opening and the two of them nearly collided at the entrance to the ladies' room. She remembered tugging the short-capped sleeves of her little black dress into place and assessing the other woman.

Nope, *she* was the other woman. After an awkward smile and nod, Kelly had scurried back to the gallery and sucked down some fruit punch the color of her cheeks. Betrayal. Lies.

Amid the crowd nibbling appetizers and sipping champagne, Peyton had found her. He cupped her elbow and whispered in her ear. "That dress should be illegal." His breath sent tingles down her spine and she fought against the sensation.

"Maybe later we can spend some time together in the main gallery. The couch is nicely cushioned."

Their backs to the wall, he'd slid his hand over the fabric of her dress and rested it on the small of her back. Even through the dress, every nerve ending in her body screamed, *Cheater. Adulteress.*

*This man is not yours,* her mind told her. She'd become, unwittingly, the woman she swore she'd never be. Every kiss they'd shared, every embrace, every night spent together had come at a cost she didn't realize she was paying.

Kelly stared at the cover of the closed journal. But she wasn't like Mary Gray. Mary had stepped, knowingly, into a relationship outside of her marriage vows. She could have said no, could have sent Esteban away, even though each cell of her cried out for him.

Just as part of Kelly cried out for Peyton now. If only, if only . . . She thought she had purged the rest of him from her system, and retreating into hiding had done that, for a while. Of course, Jonna had to be the one to figure out the connection between Kelly and Peyton, plus Peyton's acceptance of Kelly's bid for the ancient woven rugs found in what was once Gaul. Then Jonna had run straight to the top administrators of the Boston Fine Arts Museum and spilled the whole sorry tale.

*God, please don't let my wrongdoing continue to follow me like this.* Kelly remembered whispered prayers as a young teen, prayers with Lottie for the man she'd one day marry, would give herself to. Maybe that was another reason she'd avoided Lottie. God had blessed her with a family, and she'd let them down. Not only had she given Peyton her once carefully guarded innocence, but she'd given herself to a liar.

Tom wiped his brow and surveyed the kitchen floor. Bamboo hardwood. More than he could afford if he owned his own home. Winthrop had the bucks, and so far the guy's checks cleared, for which he was thankful. He shifted from his knees, then moved over to the air compressor and turned it off. Another pair of hands could have helped him get the floor set down, but so far he'd done fine on his own, slower but steady.

When Kelly dropped him off at the Winthrops' place, he almost asked her to meet him back here for lunch. Instead, he said, "See you around five."

She left him with a wave and a sunshiny smile, off to work on her old quilt.

He'd snooped around online out of curiosity to see how much she could be making on a job like that. The amount ranged from five grand to a cool twenty-five thousand. All that for scraps of fabric that someone had cared nothing about for years. Why throw money at something like that? He shook his head. Sure, he was glad for Kelly benefiting from the project. She'd had a hard life and it sounded like some tough breaks recently that she wouldn't tell him about.

He could respect that. He'd had his own tough breaks and wasn't eager to spill his guts. Tom stepped carefully on the bare subfloor and headed for his work table, where his bottled water waited for him. That, and a container of leftovers his mother had sent home with him the other night.

As he chowed down, his mind drifted back to his pastor's message on Sunday morning, about God's ways. *God's ways aren't like ours. We try to understand things that are beyond our human comprehension. How can we give and receive more in return? How can turning the cheek be rewarded? How can a servant be the greatest of all? How can God bring order out of chaos in our lives?*

Tom wanted to holler, "That last one is the million-dollar question, Pastor." He remembered long ago being read the first chapter of Genesis. "And the earth was without form and void, and darkness hovered over the face of the deep. And God said, 'Let there be light, and there was light.'" One sentence, one command was all it took. He still begged for that one command from above to produce something in his own life.

Yet Pastor's words continued replaying in his brain. "So many people ask God for His will in their lives when they should be asking God what He's doing in this world and joining in on what He's doing."

*What are you doing, God?* Somber thought for lunchtime. Sometimes Tom couldn't see what God was doing. No, a lot of the time he couldn't see it. At least he wasn't doing nothing with his time. He earned a decent paycheck working at Gray House, and this newest job would help his savings account.

"Hello, hello," a voice boomed as the front door opened. "How's my kitchen floor coming?"

"It's right on track, Dave," Tom said as Dave Winthrop entered the dining room. He carried a manila folder and hummed a tune.

"My wife is going to love this. Bamboo is so 'green,' as they say, and will last a long time." Winthrop stopped at the kitchen threshold. "Nice work, good attention to detail."

"Thank you. I'm enjoying the work. If all goes well, I'll start on the rest of the downstairs this week."

"Great job." Winthrop slapped his palm with the folder he carried. "I brought something for you."

"What's that?"

"Your family tree," Winthrop said, "or at least part of it."

"Really? Wow." Tom's stomach rumbled, but he ignored it. Once Winthrop was gone, he could grab lunch.

"Easy-peasy." Winthrop handed him the folder with a flourish. "Here's part of your family's history, all the way back a hundred and fifty years or so, on your father's side. Census records, mostly. Easy to find."

Tom opened the folder. Inside were printed copies of hand-written census records, plus a few other copies of old-looking papers. "Thank you. I told you my father doesn't talk much about his side of the family. His dad died young, and he was raised by an aunt when his mother walked out on the family." He hadn't intended to say that much. Last time Winthrop had asked about Tom's family, Tom had only said he didn't know much about either side other than they'd been in New Bedford "forever" and were pretty much a blue-collar family.

"You'll see the census records name heads of household, spouses, and children with ages. They go back every ten years or so."

Tom studied the top page. There was his name with the 2010 census. His parents were listed, too. He paged back to 1950. There was his pop, listed as twelve years old. His father's name was Albert Pereira, his mother Dolores Pereira. Tom's grandfather was listed as a "carpenter," his grandmother as a "housewife."

Carpenter, huh? A grin tugged at his mouth. So working with their hands ran in the family. "This is something else."

Winthrop nodded. "There are variations on the name some-where back there. And then one of the families has no sons to carry on the name, and . . . well, you'll see. You have a fine lineage back there. This was just the start of it."

"Thank you." Tom closed the folder and placed it on the table. "Do I owe you some money for this or something?"

"Nah." Winthrop waved off the question. "It was as easy as typing in a name and a birth date, and the paper trail revealed itself."

"Well, thank you. Thank you very much. I, uh, was just having my lunch break when you stopped by." Tom picked up his food container.

"Go right ahead. I'm passing through. I have some appointments this afternoon in Newport, but if you need anything or have questions, I'll have my cell phone on."

"All right. I'll remember that." Tom stirred his food, but didn't take a bite while Winthrop was there. "I know I'm the only one working on this, but I promise I'll get this done in good time."

"I don't doubt that. I also don't doubt that if you need a hand, you'll find one." Winthrop tapped the folder. "I hope you enjoy exploring your family history. Like I said, this is just the start."

"Thanks again." Tom nodded. "I'll have to show this to my father." Not that his father would have much interest in the family tree, but it wouldn't hurt to show him. If he liked it, fine. If not, Tom had plenty of other things to occupy his time.

Winthrop took his leave, and Tom inhaled the rest of his lunch so he could hit overdrive and get the kitchen floor finished. He turned up the music on his MP3 player dock and flipped the switch for his pneumatic nail gun. Time to get cranking and get the floor done.

He shoved his gloomy questions aside plus his curiosity about his family's records for now. The present needed his attention more than anything else. He lost himself in the cutting and measuring, then realized someone was banging on the front door.

Tom unlatched the door and pulled it open. "Kelly."

She stood on the doorstep, blinking at him. "You did say to come by at five, right?"

"Is it five already?" He hadn't finished his goal for the day. A four-foot-by-room-length patch of subfloor still lay exposed.

"Yes, it is. Almost five-thirty, actually. I tried calling you, but it went straight to voice mail."

It was bad enough she had to give him rides to the Winthrops' house, worse that she showed up and he hadn't finished what he'd hoped to accomplish that day.

"Sorry about that. I had the music turned up, didn't hear the door or the phone."

"Did you get everything finished for the day? I can come back later if you need me to."

No, he didn't need her to. "I didn't, but that's okay. I'll just work extra tomorrow."

"Is—is it something I can help you with? Do you want an extra set of hands?" She shrugged and half-smiled, as if she knew he was doing an inner boxing match with his pride.

"Actually," he said, casting a glance over his shoulder, "maybe I could use a pair of hands. I'm laying flooring. C'mon."

She followed him into the townhouse and he led her to the kitchen. "Wow," Kelly said. "This is a beautiful kitchen. I can't imagine them changing much in it."

"They had old laminate flooring that I ripped out and I'm replacing with bamboo."

She nodded, eying the nail gun. "As long as I don't have to touch that thing, I'll be glad to give you a hand."

"Okay, then." He stretched his arms. "We can knock this out in an hour if we start now."

"Just tell me what to do." Kelly grinned at him.

Maybe having to hitch a ride to the job wasn't so bad after all.

# 11

The old man summoned him early. If he were to describe his great-great-uncle's demeanor in one word, that would be giddy. He had never seen the old man giddy before.

"Look in the envelope, look," the old man said without as much as a good morning when he entered the room. "It's her. She's the one."

"She's the one what?" He'd had a sleepless night, with a sense of foreboding that something rotten was festering like last week's garbage. He pulled the papers from the envelope, unfolded them, and read.

"See. I was right about her." The old man clapped his veined, wrinkled hands.

"So what are you going to do about it?"

"Do? Nothing, at the moment. I'm not going to tell her. And neither are you." The old man spoke the last four words with the force that surprised him.

"Oh, you can be sure I won't tell her." He weighed his next words carefully. "Do you think she already knows?"

"I highly doubt it." The old man looked triumphant, as if he were prepared to kill the fatted calf.

As if he would let the old man do anything so foolish.

Kelly smiled as she woke up to the morning sun, then winced. Only ninety minutes of work helping Tom lay the flooring at the townhouse had awakened muscles in her back and legs she'd forgotten she had. But it had been fun, and definitely different from working on the quilt. They swung by a Thai restaurant and ordered takeout, which they ate at the harbor front. It almost felt like a date, but then the harbor front was neutral ground that they both agreed was relaxing. A flicker of memory, the other night at Tom's parents' home, made her recall something that had sparked between them, if only for an instant before they were interrupted. His touch on her hair had been so soft, so gentle. . . .

Kelly shook her head and sat up on the side of the bed. Another day's worth of work stretched out before her. She'd completed cutting out the blocks that needed to be replaced on all five compasses on the quilt. Now the trick was incorporating the newer fabric with the old without sacrificing any of the old fibers.

If she had truly thought about it, she should have turned the project down. But then again, she needed the money. Then there was the issue of her being the lone bidder. Kelly tried calling Mr. Chandler's office after she'd showered and dressed for her workday. His secretary said he was in meetings all day and she would leave him a message.

Her phone chimed while she was leaving her number for Mr. Chandler. Tom.

She ended the call to Mr. Chandler just in time. "Good morning, I'm almost on my way out the door."

"Hey, I'm glad I caught you. My father's dropping me off at the Winthrops' house today. So if I finish here in time, I'll end up at Gray House by mid-afternoon." Tom's voice sounded tight.

"Okay, thanks for letting me know." She was probably reading too much into it. But then the other night at the Pereiras' house, she couldn't ignore the tension between father and son, and the unspoken competition between the Pereira brothers, at least on Tom's part.

He wasn't Nick Pereira. She realized she wouldn't find him half as interesting if he were. With Tom, you didn't know what to expect, and she liked that. But on the other hand, being with him was comfortable. Last night at the harbor, she could have sat there for hours with him as the sun slid down below the horizon behind them.

"I'll see you this afternoon. If you get a moment, I have another favor to ask."

"What's that?"

"Can you check the greenhouse sprinklers and make sure the timer's not set for noon?"

"I can do that."

"See you later. Thanks." With that, he left her to her day.

She had a little more time that morning to study the first of the compasses she would soon repair. The holes had edges where the cotton fibers were unraveling. If she could only stop the unraveling and then replace the missing patch without ruining the pattern.

The quilt was rapidly becoming such a metaphor, the longer Kelly worked on it and the more she read Mary Gray's journal. Mary's life had turned into shreds, much like the quilt. But Mary's story was already told and done; there could be no reworking of her tale. The quilt, though, had hope. Kelly went down to the kitchen, her footsteps echoing off the walls. She'd developed her routine in the house of eating a simple breakfast of toast and some fruit, along with a cup of strong coffee.

Her mind still couldn't quite get used to the fact that she was the sole occupant of a home that had been vacant for who knows how long. Yes, someone had occasionally maintained the inside. She could tell that. But as far as someone living here for any real length of time? It had been decades since anyone had lived and loved inside these walls.

As the coffee brewed and the aroma filled the kitchen, Kelly found it easy to imagine the bustle of servants and cooks from years gone by. What it must have taken to maintain a place like this.

"It's a shame no one has appreciated you for so long," Kelly said aloud. Then she felt rather foolish, speaking aloud to the house. Not that she expected any kind of response besides the coffeepot gurgling.

She heard a creaking above her, as if someone walked the space above. It was the captain's bedroom, kept separate from his wife as was the custom of the time. The sound didn't make her shiver. A breeze outside was making the maple tree's branches sway. The house likely was doing some settling of its own.

Kelly knew enough not to fear noises. It was the real-live people who could hurt you, not the imaginary musings and memories.

She wondered why Mary hadn't mentioned the quilt any-more since that earlier journal entry. But then sewing was part of everyday life for most women of that time period. However, Mary had the status of a whaling captain's wife. Not quite that of a merchant, but enough to have a grand home.

After breakfast, she pulled out her magnifier and set herself to concentrating on fibers and threads for the morning.

A thumping downstairs roused her from her focus on the quilt. Between giving Tom rides, which she didn't mind, and the occasional phone call, interruptions yanked her from her flow of work. Maybe it wasn't a fast flow, but she still inched along toward her goal.

Kelly opened the front door to see a young woman about her age standing there. She wore a crisp, white blouse topped by a navy blazer, a little warm for this time of year, along with some nice khakis.

"Yes?" Had she left the front gate unlocked? She ought to check it once she got rid of this visitor. The other day when the Pereira clan had descended on Gray House, she might have forgotten and left the gate unlocked. Visitors definitely didn't help her work flow.

"I'm Megan Hughes, from the *New Bedford Star.*"

Kelly noticed for the first time an official-looking badge that hung from a lanyard. "I'm not interested in a newspaper subscription."

"Oh, I'm not here about a subscription." Megan looked as hopeful as a hound dog trying to catch a scent somewhere beyond Kelly's shoulder. "I've been driving by the house for a few months now, and it looks to me like someone is trying to work on restoring the outside."

"Yes, there's a groundskeeper who has been working on the gardens. Except he's not here right now." Kelly's instincts made her want to close the door in the woman's face, but so far the reporter had been polite. Plus, nothing would make a reporter persist more than a closed door.

"So is this your house? When did you move in? I don't remember anyone ever living here," said Megan.

"No, it's not my house. I'm . . .." She wasn't sure how much to tell the young woman. Mr. Chandler had never told her *not* to talk to the press. It's not like she was here working on a top-secret project. "The house is owned by a private company. I'm here on-site working on a commission to restore a textile project."

"Okay. I figured it might be owned by an absentee owner or even a company of some kind, which made me wonder seeing you living here." Megan whipped out a note pad and started scribbling. "So, I imagine the period pieces in this house are amazing."

"They are." Kelly nodded. She decided to give her a tidbit of information. "I'm actually working on restoring an old quilt that was sewn by the wife of the house's first owner."

"Really, you don't say? Now, I would love to see that." Megan nodded. "Our readers would love the human interest angle of the story. Do you mind if I see it?"

"Well, I should talk with the house's owner about that. I'm really quite busy right now and it's not finished," Kelly explained. "I expect to be done by the end of the summer."

"Here's my card." The reporter fished a business card from her jacket pocket. "If the company clears you to talk about the quilt, call me. Like I said, I think it'll make a good story. With photos."

"Thank you, Ms. Hughes." Kelly studied the business card. "I'll let you know."

She tried not to sigh as she closed the door while the reporter left the way she came. She frowned at her phone. She'd definitely have to call Mr. Chandler and let him know about the inquisitive Ms. Hughes. Maybe she'd get his voice mail and she could leave a quick yet succinct message.

His receptionist put her right through, and he answered after the first ring. "Ms. Frost."

"I'm calling you because a reporter stopped by today, asking about what's been going on here at Gray House this summer."

"And you told her nothing, I presume?"

"I told her someone's been working on the garden and that I've been working on the quilt—"

"You shouldn't have said anything."

"She didn't seem to be the kind to take no for an answer. If I hadn't given her a little bit of information, she might not have left." Her own chutzpah surprised her, but then, she'd dealt with uptight museum people before, why not deal with an uptight lawyer, or manager, or whatever title Mr. Chandler had?

For a few seconds, she thought the call had been dropped, but when she glanced at her phone, the line was still keeping time. "Mr. Chandler?"

"You're probably right. Did she leave any contact information?"

"She did. I told her I'd pass it along to you." Kelly ambled along toward the ballroom. "If that was okay."

"Yes, yes. You did right. What is her phone number, please?"

Kelly gave him the number.

"If she contacts you again, call me."

"I'll do that." She stared at her now-silent phone. Weird encounter. She went back to the quilt, donned her gloves and resumed the posture of leaning over the object and resuming her work.

Kelly shook her head. If the reporter returned, it would be because Mr. Chandler allowed it. She couldn't imagine that happening, from his tone. She hunkered down and focused on the first star-shaped compass until the light from the windows started to dim.

⁂

Thanks to Kelly's help, the kitchen floor was now complete. Tom spent the day working on trim work, then measured the living area again. This would take longer, with more angles and cuts. The stacked boxes of flooring loomed in the entry-way of the townhouse.

A firm knock sounded on the door. Pop, who said he'd be glad to give him a ride to his apartment. Via his parents' house for supper again. He hadn't been to the grocery store in about a week, so this time he wouldn't turn them down.

He could probably talk to his father about the genealogy that Dave Winthrop had given him, too. Maybe that was one way to bridge the yawning gap between them.

"You ready to go, Son?" Pop wasn't given to waiting.

"I just need to turn off some lights and lock up." He turned off the kitchen light and unplugged his tools. He made sure he grabbed the folder from Winthrop.

"The floor looks good. What kind of wood is that?"

"Bamboo."

"You don't say." Pop shook his head. "I never would have thought."

"It's very durable and 'green,'" Tom said as he motioned toward the entryway.

"Green, shmeen." Pop waved. "We were reusing things for building construction years ago. That's nothing new. So what if they call a fancy flooring material 'green'?"

Tom chuckled. "I know. But it's still a nice floor."

"That it is." Pop shuffled as he stepped closer to his car. When had he started to shuffle like that? A flash of memory came to Tom, of Pop tossing the football around with him and Nick, the three of them tumbling into the leaves as the brothers took turns trying to tackle their father.

They were on their way, zooming along through the city traffic. Pop muttered at drivers as they careened along the streets. Tom held on to the armrest until they pulled into his parents' driveway. He would almost rather risk driving himself than riding with his father. Twenty-five days until his next MRI. No more headaches since his trip to the ER. He should be grateful, and he was. But that didn't make the time pass any more quickly.

It was just him and his parents for supper. Bella was busy with her summer job and had plans with friends, or so Mom said.

"She's just taking off with her life." Mom picked up the last of the supper dishes. "Broke the news to us today that she's planning to be in Europe next summer, on an internship before her senior year."

"Wow. Really?" His baby sister was going places. Literally. He never thought she'd get past that silly-girl phase, raving over her newest purse or pair of shoes, exclaiming over the latest news from her reality shows.

"She says she's going to change the world someday." His mother chuckled.

"I think she needs to finish her degree first," said his father. "Can't get anywhere without an education, or some kind of job training. Might as well be stuck doing odd jobs or working fast food or a desk job. How can someone support themselves on that?"

"Oh, honey, she's going to finish college. This is just in between semesters and will look good on her résumé." His mother headed off to the kitchen. Tom figured that within seconds, the coffee would be brewing.

"Well, she'd better."

"Uh, Pop, I have something to show you. Dave Winthrop brought me a folder of information about our family today." He might as well dive in now and see what his father's reaction would be, if he had any type of reaction to his family's history. He slid the folder across the table toward his pop.

"Dave Winthrop?"

"The owner of the townhouse where I'm installing the new wood and tile floors."

"Ah, okay." He reached for the folder. "So he put some family information in this folder, huh?"

Tom nodded. "I always wondered about Grandpa Pereira, you know."

"Yes, I know. You used to drive me crazy when you were about Hunter's age, doing some family-tree project for school." Pop opened the folder, then slipped on his reading glasses.

"I did?"

Pop nodded. "You chased me around for over a week, asking me about relatives I hadn't thought about since I was a kid."

"Well, Winthrop is a genealogy buff. He went back quite a few generations. I didn't realize we'd been in New Bedford that long."

"Lots of census records here and birth certificates." Pop shuffled the papers. "Some good hardworking folks on those lists."

"But you never talked about them."

"No. What's done is done. I didn't see the point, then you kids got too busy to care. Besides, my father's family isn't around. Just me and your great-aunt." Pop ran his fingers across the pages. "Look at us, going back across the years. Birth certificates and death records. and the census. All the way till before the Civil War. We must've lost a few family members then." His father passed a page to him from the 1870 census, then the 1860 census.

"Hector and Leticia Delgado, with seven children: Leonora, eighteen; Isabel, sixteen; Tomás, twelve; Hortensia, ten; Lupe, nine; and Pedro, seven." His father rested his hand on the pages. "It says Hector was a shipbuilder."

"So Hector is your great-great-great-grandfather?"

"I think that's right. Pedro, the youngest, was my great-great-grandfather." His father sighed. "Not much in the way of genealogy in my house. Your great-aunt worked hard to take care of me after my own papa died. We worked at just getting by."

"Why didn't you go to college, Pop?" He ventured the question, something he'd never asked before.

"I wasn't a good student. Dyslexic. I was labeled a dummy and sent to special classes." His father's head hung low. "No one ever mentioned college to me. At least I went to trade school. I was able to give you and your mother a good life, keep food on the table for you kids."

No wonder his pop had hounded them all along about education, education, education. No wonder his pop had a cow when Tom entered the Army two summers after high school, then relented a little when he learned about the GI Bill benefits Tom would earn.

"I didn't know you were dyslexic, too."

Mom entered the dining room, the scent of freshly brewing coffee following her. "Your pop never wanted to say anything. He didn't think it would make much difference to you."

"Of course it would have." All these years he'd struggled in school, and his mother had been the one to go to the special meetings for his IEP in the Special Education Department. An "individualized education plan," which had helped him graduate, just barely. He wouldn't have felt so alone. But Tom didn't bother saying these things aloud.

"I'm ashamed, Tom. Ashamed I passed this to you. Which is why I wanted you to go beyond what I did and not let it hold you back. Then when you got hurt in the Army—" Pop's voice cut off. Mom reached for his hand.

"Pop, it's not your fault. Really, it's not." Tom cleared his throat. "I've been asking God what's going on, what His purpose is in all this, and what I'm supposed to do. I don't hold you responsible at all."

"But still, I know learning disabilities get passed down in the family."

"That's true," Mom said. "But Tom can do a great many things. Can't you, Tommy?"

"Pretty much." Tom shrugged. "All except drive, for now."

"Have you had any more headaches?" His mother's forehead wrinkled.

"Nah, not really. Only if I get overtired. But I've been okay."

"Well, you need to take good care of yourself. I think it's awfully sweet, too, that Kelly is helping you out."

"She's a . . . neat person" was all he could manage to say.

"A 'neat person'?" Mom shook her head. "Really, you can do better than that. I think you should keep her around. I like her a lot. Seems like a lost, sad soul who's finding her way back from wherever she's been."

Tom nodded. He should be grateful that the focus was off him. He hadn't intended his own issues to be the topic of conversation, but at least it wasn't with the rest of the family around. That, and the topic of Kelly Frost. How to keep her around, he didn't know.

The other night at the harbor, he'd fought to restrain himself and managed to not give her a quick kiss, which had almost occurred the night he'd brought her home for dinner. Watching her face, lit by a glow from the twilight reflected on the water, as she talked about some of the places she'd traveled in her work, well, he almost couldn't pay attention to her stories. When she dropped the self-conscious shell, Kelly Frost glowed.

What had life done to her to scar her so much, living in a foster home aside? It sounded like the last home she'd lived in had almost become the family she never had.

"Son, you okay?" Mom patted him on the arm and offered him a cup of coffee. "You were off somewhere for a bit."

"I'm okay." He accepted the cup of coffee and took a sip. "I was just thinking. Pop, I'm looking into some horticulture or

**123**

woodworking classes at the community college. They have a good program that helps veterans, so this fall you might be looking at a college student."

"Is that so?" Pop's voice brightened as he closed the folder labeled Pereira genealogy.

# 12

Kelly opened her eyes, fabric inches away from her eyelashes. Somehow, during the afternoon she'd drifted off while working on the quilt. She shifted her arms to push herself upright, but the sensation of knives slicing through her neck and upper shoulders made her stop. She forced herself to move and moaned at the pain, reaching for the quilt top fabric with her gloved hands. Good. She hadn't drooled on it or laid her bare skin on the piece. What had happened to her energy?

The light outside had faded at last. Another muscle spasm shot through her right shoulder as she glanced toward the hallway. Somehow, she had to get herself out of the chair, away from the ballroom, then up the stairs to her bathroom and the deep claw foot tub.

She'd overdone it. She squinted at the stitches she'd worked on this afternoon. No good. The new threads had already started unraveling the weakened fibers. Just what she hadn't wanted to happen.

Today's work, all nine hours or so of it, had been for nothing.

That knowledge didn't help the lancing pain that made her gasp for breath when she stood. She should have known better. Take her time. She wasn't about to call Jonna for help, or anyone else.

When Kelly reached the ballroom doorway, she leaned on the pocket door frame, taking slow deep breaths.

One step at a time. She could do this. As she walked, fresh pain sliced down her back in spasms, toward her knees. Maybe raising her arms up over her head would help.

She paused again and tried the maneuver. Bolts of pain struck her shoulders and she lowered her arms. She'd gone and done it good, this time. A whimper escaped her lips before she could bite it back.

Finally, she reached the stairs and tried the first step. One at a time, she could do it as long as she could stand hunched over the railing as she made her way to the top. With her phone finally tucked onto the bureau beside Mary Gray's journal, Kelly hobbled to the bathroom and managed to get a hot bath started. She didn't have any salts, but figured the hot water alone would help.

She found her pajamas and a fresh towel and laid them aside for later, then sank into the hot water, hissing as she did so. Bringing medicines hadn't been on her mind when moving into Gray House. She doubted the place had a first aid kit, although she hadn't taken the time to explore for things like that. She'd been too busy.

Kelly slowly worked her muscles, still wincing at the dull ache that shot through her shoulders. Her hands cramped as well. Carpal tunnel syndrome wouldn't be too far away if she didn't keep up with her exercises.

Maybe today's overdoing it would be a minor setback. The fraying threads of the old quilt pattern told her she still had plenty of work ahead of her. She'd never walked away from a job and wasn't about to with this one, foolhardy as it was to try to restore the quilt. If she'd really thought about it, she should have rejected the bid request and held out for something else.

But someone had wanted her here. A door slammed somewhere below. The noise made her jump involuntarily, causing another gasp.

That was it. She crawled from the tub and pulled on her robe. No weapon, but her phone. Kelly didn't know what or who made this particular noise, but she was ready.

She called directory assistance for the non-emergency 911 number for the New Bedford Police. "Yes, I'm at 248 County Street, alone. I heard a noise, and I'm afraid someone was trying to get into the house." The dispatcher assured her they'd send a car to patrol by the house and check the yard for her.

Maybe she should have called 911, but then, if it were nothing she'd feel mighty foolish. Her feet leaving damp footprints on the floor, she descended the main staircase. Another bang, from the rear of the house. Kelly tightened her grip on the phone and padded as silently as possible toward the kitchen. Tomorrow, she was going to find a baseball bat or something to keep on hand. Or pepper spray.

The back door was ajar, with the breeze banging the screen door against the rear of the house. Kelly opened the back door and pulled the screen door shut, locking it from the inside, then doing the same with the main door.

Had someone been in the house with her? Tom had come and gone already with his other job, his father giving him a ride. She'd remembered to check the sprinkler timer, and it was correctly set for six a.m. Maybe that was it. She was to blame for not making sure the old kitchen door latched.

Firm pounding sounded toward the front of the house. Kelly moved that direction as quickly as she could with aching shoulders, back, and neck. She unlatched the front door to see a New Bedford police officer on the front steps with a patrol car at the curb. She could glimpse a rear fender through the iron gate.

"Miss, you called about the noise?" The young officer strained to look over her shoulder. "I need to see some identification, please."

Kelly presented him with her driver's license, as the dispatcher had suggested she have it ready. "Yes, I did. It seems silly now that I called, but like I said, I'm staying here alone and heard some noises." She felt like an idiot now, playing the proverbial helpless female scaredy-cat.

"That's quite all right, Ms. Frost." The officer nodded. "I'm going to go around the side of the house and look through the back yard, if you don't mind."

"Not at all."

"I'm on until eleven p.m., so I'll try to swing by once more before my shift is over."

"Thanks, officer . . ."

"Dudden."

"Officer Dudden, I appreciate it." She smiled and nodded at the man, then relatched the front door and checked the back door once more. It had never occurred to her to check the windows for locks. She shuddered as she headed upstairs.

Kelly winced as before while hauling herself upstairs. If this was what getting old felt like, she was in no hurry. She reached her bedroom and stopped at the bureau.

Something was off about Mary Gray's journal. She hadn't moved it, but she knew she'd set it directly on the lace doily without any hanging off the edge of the fabric. Now one whole corner of the journal hung over the wood.

Had it been moved?

Her arms prickled as if she suddenly stood in a full breeze. Ridiculous. She'd been in a hurry to get downstairs, and she hadn't even paid much attention to the journal. Maybe she'd even bumped it when grabbing her phone on the way downstairs.

Either way, she didn't like it. She'd call Mrs. Acres in the morning and share her concerns about the house's security.

After a light supper, she settled down to read Mary Gray's story once again. She winced as she sat down on the uphol-stered cushion. If this pain and the muscle spasms didn't quit, she'd hunt down a massage therapist.

---

*August 5, 1851*

*Esteban returned to the house for another lesson, he said. At last, after a long absence. But it is he who has taught me a new lan-guage, the language of love for the past three days. While I was once the teacher, I have become his pupil. I sent the help to their homes and we have scarcely left my room, but to care for little Hiram. I am doomed. When Hiram returns from the sea, I shall leave him. Scandal or no. Esteban is my love, my world. May God have mercy on us.*

---

Kelly's cheeks burned as she closed the journal. She almost wanted to take another bath after reading Mary's entry. The woman had said plenty without sharing details. Her remark about asking for God's mercy sounded hollow.

"You can never beg God to have mercy on sin, but only on the repentant sinner," Lottie had said once upon a time, when Kelly had called during graduate school.

Kelly put the journal away, this time in a nightstand drawer near the bed. She had earned the right to hear Mary's story by working on her quilt, but she wasn't sure she wanted to keep reading.

Mary didn't sound exactly repentant, but more as if she couldn't help herself. Rationalizing. Didn't everyone do that from time to time? When does wrong become right, when does the "these are my feelings and I can't help myself" make things wrong in the sight of the law and of God, the Lawgiver?

Kelly's own indiscretions came back to her mind, although they were never far away. She should have known something wasn't quite right with the whole relationship with Peyton. The way it was always the two of them, never anyone else. Only calling him on his cell phone, never the office. She had assumed it would keep things from getting into a professional snarl for both of them.

Oh, it had avoided a snarl all right. Avoided his wife and their colleagues from knowing until Jonna had stumbled onto the truth.

*Lord, I should have known, should have realized.* But she'd been naive and giddy with the prospect of a future with Peyton.

She'd even asked him once about when they could go public with their relationship.

"Soon," he'd told her. "I'm waiting for the right time for both of us." Then he'd whisked her to Martha's Vineyard for a weekend, and she'd put the idea out of her mind.

Mary, Mary. Kelly patted the nightstand. She decided to drag herself to the nearest drugstore to get some ibuprofen. Maybe the medication would soothe her muscles so she could sleep tonight. Sleep, without thoughts of Mary Gray inside her head.

A blue service van marked A-1 Security Systems was parked in front of Gray House, with William Chandler's car behind it.

"Oh good, they're here," Kelly said from the driver's seat.

"You don't sound like that's good." Tom wished she'd have called him the other night. He would have camped out on the front steps, or something, just to ensure her safety.

She maneuvered her car into the space at the back entrance of the property. "Good, as in I'll sleep better with a security system in place."

"What?"

Kelly didn't answer, but parked the car and got out.

William Chandler appeared near the driver's side door and was already talking when Tom closed his own door. "—overreacting."

"What's your supervisor's number, or your boss's number?" Kelly stood beside the car, her hands on her hips. "Surely you have a boss. I'd think he or she would want to protect what's inside the house, and I'm honestly surprised they don't have a security system in place already. There are thousands of dollars of valuable antiques and textiles in that house."

Chandler stood there, looking like he was about to say a few choice words himself. Then Tom caught his eye and he backed down. "My 'supervisor or boss' can't be bothered. He's a very busy man. This house is only one of his interests and is hardly at the top of his real estate list."

"I would think if you had someone living here in a house that had been empty for so long, you'd want to take a few precautions," Tom said, giving Kelly a nod. "Haven't you heard of real estate squatters who take over abandoned or empty houses? Except this one's not empty anymore."

"I can't believe you phoned the police over noises." Chandler shook his head.

Didn't the guy have a clue? Tom opened his mouth to say something, but Kelly beat him to it.

"Who should I have called? You? Would you have come out and checked the house for me?" Kelly shook her head, then took a deep breath. "Look, honestly, I'm not trying to cause problems. I'm just here to work on the quilt. Which is coming along, in case you were wondering."

Footsteps on the lawn made them look toward the house. The serviceman approached, holding a clipboard. "Mr. Chandler?"

With that, Kelly headed toward the house, Tom following.

"Hey," he said, falling into step beside her.

"I'm a little cranky this morning, I'm warning you. I think someone was in the house last night, my neck and shoulders are killing me, and I've hardly slept." She paused at the back steps and faced him.

"You should have called me last night," he said.

"But how would you have gotten over here?"

"I would have figured something out. Either that, or had someone come for you. My parents have an extra room you could have crashed in."

"Thanks, that's really nice of you." She gave him half a smile.

He couldn't figure out what was with her. Sometimes she opened up like the morning sun coming from behind the clouds and it made him stop and stare. Other times like now, she acted as if they'd only just met.

"If it helps you to know, I'm not a fan of Chandler, either. But I have a job and I like it. I want to keep it." His words surprised him, about liking the job. But the realization was true.

"Me too, me too." She opened the back door, and winced.

"Are you okay?"

"I overdid it a little, sat too long without stretching." She stood in the doorway, looking down at him.

"Ah." He took the plunge. "There's a jazz fest tonight at the harbor park. I need a ride."

"Oh. You do?"

"Think you can take a night off from this big old house?"

Now a full smile crept across her face. "I think I can."

"Pick me up at seven?" He never imagined he'd be glad to be the one waiting on a ride.

"I'll be there."

# 13

*December 1851*

*One year ago, I cradled an infant. Little Hiram walks the floors of Gray House now as the child inside me grows. Esteban's child. No one else knows and that is as it should be. I shall tell Esteban soon, if he has not surmised my state already. He stays at the house now, away from the eyes of the servants. I have let all but one couple go. My funds are short and the others' prying eyes I could not risk betraying us.*

*Mrs. Walter Woodhouse came calling, telling me she has missed seeing me these many weeks at a church service. It used to be that I would walk to the house of God with my neighbors on the block, or we would proceed carriage by carriage. Those holy halls have no place for me now. Others may enter with clean attire and sin-filled hearts inside, but I know better. At least I am honest with my state as an adulteress. I have taken to heading to the lookout to see if Hiram's ship is returning. At one time he said spring, he hoped.*

Kelly set the journal down and covered her mouth with her hand. Oh, Mary. She shouldn't have been surprised at this turn in the lady's story. Maybe it wasn't fair. Times were different back then, and people didn't marry for love, but for money, convenience, companionship, or part of a business transaction. And then, were you to meet someone that you "connected with . . ."

She shoved the thought aside. It was modern thinking, "connecting with" someone. But Mary and Esteban had definitely connected. Call it the hormones of youth spurred on by loneliness. Still, Mary had taken vows. She should have known better. Generations were affected by her and Esteban's actions.

Kelly glanced at her phone. She'd knocked off work early, listening to her aching muscles and tired body. She had time yet before getting ready to take Tom to the jazz festival. Not a date, she reminded herself. Just two friends, enjoying some time together. She needed to learn to have more fun. Sometimes the instinct for survival drowned out the fun.

She picked up the journal again and focused on Mary's story.

*April 1852*

*On a stormy night with Steban at my side, I gave birth to another son. Wild dark hair like his father's, skin fairer than his father's and more like mine. I cannot think of what the future holds. Esteban tells me that we will find a way, somehow, to be together. Yet I cannot leave my little Hiram behind. Two brothers, one darker, one lighter. I see no resolution, but Esteban says to be patient. We name our little one Peter, or Pedro.*

*August 1852*

*The news I once longed for and now dread has arrived: a letter from Hiram. Its passionless instructions tell me that I should expect him by the time the leaves fall from the trees. I cry myself to sleep every night in the security of Steban's arms. He has thought of a plan, but I do not like it. We can tell him of our intentions, without telling him of little Peter. His youngest brother is but two years old, and his mother is used to caring for a brood of children. The Delgados are good people. He will take Peter to his mother, who will care for him without question, until he and I can settle things with Hiram.*

The shadows in the sitting room were long. Kelly sniffled, then brushed the tears from her cheeks. Mary, giving up her child. She set the journal on the small round table, the words on the page. *He will take Peter to his mother.*

What must Esteban's mother have thought, seeing her son carrying an infant through the door, and placing him in her arms? Did she love him like one of her own? Esteban had mentioned to Mary that his mother still had small children in the home, which might be possible, if Esteban had been in his early twenties when Peter, or Pedro, was born.

There truly was nothing new under the sun. Parents failed their children, children were removed from homes to grow up somewhere else because of their parents' failures. Kelly had always thought she was on the outside, as were her fellow foster siblings. They didn't really have a "home," like in the Hallmark movies.

She used to dream about having a mother and a father, sitting around the table at Thanksgiving and Christmas, having cousins come to visit. Family vacations, road trips in the car. Slumber parties.

One night Lottie had found her in tears, around age fourteen or so. She hadn't been invited to someone's party at school. Her hand-me-down jeans and off-brand sneakers hadn't passed the fashion muster, so she'd been excluded from the "inner circle."

"I don't feel like I belong, Lottie," she'd wailed. "Even if my clothes were the right kind, I still think they'd laugh me off." But it was more than not belonging because of clothes.

"You belong in the best way possible," Lottie had said. She stroked her hair. "I know it hurts and I wish I could make it stop. You're part of God's family and you are never alone, and you never have to worry if your clothes are just right."

No easy choice then, or now. Life hadn't dealt Mary Gray the hand she'd expected, and Kelly had learned a long time ago not to expect too much. She was sorry for her unbelief, probably more than Mary was about her goings-on with Esteban.

She made herself cut the pity party short. Lottie had always talked about counting her blessings. Right now, Kelly figured she ought to do the same. A good place to stay, plenty of work for the moment, her needs met. She had people who loved her, even if that group was small. She had some new friends she liked—a lot, especially Tom. Her face flushed. The past was just that—past.

Time to pick out some clothes for this evening. The sun had baked the outside with midsummer heat, but with the lengthening shadows, a breeze drifted through the open window.

Her phone buzzed, an unfamiliar number, but she took the call.

"Ms. Frost, this is Megan Hughes, the reporter from the *New Bedford Star*."

"I remember you."

"I'm calling to let you know that Firstborn Holdings has approved my interview with you, so I can see the quilt and have a tour of the house."

"Oh, I'm not sure I'm prepared for a tour."

"That's all right. A Mr. Plummer is supposed to meet me at the house and give me the tour. We've set it up for next Tuesday at eleven a.m., if that works for you, too."

"My schedule is flexible, so that's fine."

"Wonderful. I'll see you then."

After the call ended, Kelly stared at the phone. Mr. Plummer? What about Chandler? Well, it shouldn't surprise her that the company would send someone a little more personable. At least, though, they weren't depending on her to give a tour.

---

Tom closed his eyes and listened to the music echoing off the harbor. Kelly sat beside him on a lawn chair that he'd found while scrounging in the tool shed on his property. He hadn't thought he'd need them at the time, but now he realized the convenient turn of insignificant events.

"That was beautiful," Kelly said as the last strains of the song drifted away. She smiled at him. "I'm glad I came tonight."

"Me too. A change of scenery is a good thing sometimes, my mom likes to say."

"She's right." Kelly took a deep breath, then exhaled. "I guess they're going for an intermission right now?"

"It looks that way." He studied her face. "So, what's up? You look like you want to say something."

She shrugged. "I've been reading Mary Gray's diary. I can't stop thinking about it. I got to the part tonight where she had an illegitimate son by a young carpenter she was tutoring in English."

Tom shook his head. "Wow. I wonder if that's in the records officially anywhere."

"I don't know. It would be interesting to find out. It's sad, really. She ended up letting her lover's family take the baby while she dealt with her husband's return. And get this, the guy's family is Portuguese." Kelly shifted on the seat, slowly, as if giving her muscles a chance to stretch.

"I bet Dave Winthrop would know where to look." At her questioning glance, he continued. "The bamboo floor guy."

"Oh, that's right. But how would he know where to look?"

"He's really into genealogy," Tom replied. "He's traced my pop's side of the family back to the 1850s. When I get a chance, I might start looking farther back, to see when they first came to the United States."

She nodded. "That's neat, that you have that history you can search through."

Ah. Tom remembered about Kelly's family tree, or lack thereof. "It was easier than I thought it would be. Winthrop found some census records."

She looked as though she was going to say something else, then stopped. He let the silence fall between them, with sounds of the harbor and other concertgoers swirling around their self-imposed bubble.

"Are you almost through with the job on that townhouse?"

"One more day, tomorrow. Then it's back to Gray House full time."

"I'm glad." Her face flushed, she glanced down at her lap.

"Walk with me for a few minutes?" He stood, his legs reminding him he'd been sitting still for too long. If he stretched his legs, his back might not flare up and he'd be grateful to get out of bed in the morning.

"Sure." They left the lawn chairs and ambled closer to the water. "What did you think you'd find, looking back at your family?"

"I don't know. I haven't looked more closely at it yet. The census records show I've got a long line of hardworking people behind me." He stopped at the edge of the pier that ran the length of the waterfront.

"That's something to be proud of." She smiled at him, then glanced toward the harbor waters with sad eyes.

He nudged her shoulder with his own, not wanting to risk anything more than casual. "I bet you have something special back in your family tree."

"I've never cared to look."

"Well, you should. I mean, just because your parents were, ah . . ." He couldn't find the right word, but didn't want to say anything like "failures" since he didn't really know much about them, other than their daughter lived in foster care for a good chunk of her younger years.

"Failures, losers." Kelly glanced back at him. "I've said those words and others before. I honestly don't know if I want to look back to see what I can find. I never met my grand-parents, either side, that I remember. Or maybe I did, once. Mom stopped at a pretty house, somewhere south of Boston. She, ah, she walked me to the front door and we knocked. She asked the lady at the door for some money and asked if she wanted to meet me. I think it was her mother."

"What happened?"

Kelly shrugged. "We went inside, and the lady gave me a glass of milk and a Pop-Tart. I really don't remember much of what they talked about, but I know she gave my mother some money before we left. We never went back again, once my mother got another boyfriend." She crossed her arms and rubbed away a shiver. "Jenks didn't want Mom to have any-thing to do with anyone but him. Our house was a prison until Mom died." Her voice had grown tight.

"I'm sorry. I can't imagine living like that."

Kelly shook her head. "No, I'm sorry. I shouldn't have said anything. Here, you invite me to this beautiful evening, and I'm spouting off a bunch of ick."

He drew on his courage and allowed himself to slip his arm around her waist. "I like Kelly Frost, spouting off and all. God

**140**

knows I've done enough spouting myself, it's a wonder people would want to be around me sometimes."

She leaned against him, but kept her arms around herself. "You're not so bad."

"Ha. You missed the worst of it."

"Really. I admire your courage, after what you've been through."

He caught a whiff of her shampoo, something like fresh flowers. "I'm a work in progress. I'll just be glad when I can get cleared to drive again. A couple of weeks."

"I'm glad you needed a ride tonight."

"Me too. And I'm glad you're the one who brought me." He surprised himself by turning his head toward her and planting a kiss on the top of her head.

"Now, you can do better than that." Kelly slid her arm around him, then pulled him close for a quick kiss on the lips.

———

The old man was getting his way again. He'd never before allowed anyone into the house, not until Ms. Frost. And with the latest news, the old man had been quite feisty. The visiting physician said he was making a remarkable comeback, something that none of them had expected.

It certainly wasn't boding well for his own personal wallet. After all these years, after all he'd done, his own future was changing faster than his stock portfolio, which had taken a hit in the last few years.

The old man had better come through in the end. Otherwise, he didn't know what he was going to do.

# 14

"You have certainly had your work cut out for you, no pun intended," said Megan Hughes as she studied the quilt, spread out on the tables in the ballroom.

Kelly nodded. "Because of the damage and neglect over the years, and the natural process of aging, it's been quite a job. So far I've completed repairs on three of the five compasses, as much as I can. I have two stars to complete, then the background, and I'm going to attach a new binding to the edges." She frowned. There was really nothing else she could do for the piece, but it irked her to have to add so much new to the old.

"So how long have you been working in this business?"

"Not counting my undergraduate internships, I've been full time for nearly seven years."

"And you've worked for some familiar names? The Boston Fine Arts Museum, for starters."

Kelly nodded and tried not to flinch. "Yes, there was a two-year project we wrapped up about six months ago."

"Now, when did you receive notice about the job here at Gray House?" Megan's pen scribbled furiously on a notepad.

"It was in May, and that's when I first came out here to see the quilt." It seemed like years ago, and not mere months.

A knock sounded at the front door. Megan stopped writing long enough to glance at her phone. "I'll bet that's Mr. Plummer from the company. He's going to give a tour of the house."

Kelly nodded, for the first time in weeks feeling like an outsider here. She'd grown accustomed to the house's noises and knew the halls well enough to go through them in the dark—not that she'd try it. Having the new security system helped her peace of mind, too.

Kelly was the one to get the door. She opened it to see an old man, propped up against a rolling walker. A young woman stood behind him, looking efficient yet ready to hover over him if needed.

"Mr. Plummer?"

He nodded. "Ms. Frost. May I come in?"

"Of course. Come in. The reporter is in the ballroom already and I've been showing her the quilt."

With a heave of the walker and a grunt, Mr. Plummer waved off both Kelly's assistance and that of his official assistant, nurse, or whoever she was.

"Tara, you can wait here in the front sitting room." Mr. Plummer waved her toward the front room.

"But, Mister—"

"No 'but Mister.' Ms. Frost looks strong enough to catch me if I start to topple over." His words had a bite to them, but Kelly caught a glimmer in the old man's eyes.

"Of course." Tara the assistant skittered into the sitting room.

"Now, show me the way, and show me what you've been doing with my quilt."

"Your quilt?"

"Yes, I'm the CEO of Firstborn Holdings. Jonas Plummer."

She froze. CEO? "Nice to meet you."

"Don't lie, young lady. I'm sure you don't think it's very nice to meet me and you probably have dozens of questions to ask me."

At that, she did laugh. "I wasn't lying, just being polite. And you're right, I do have some questions for you." This man was a switch from Mr. Chandler, a good switch.

He leaned on his rolling walker, stopping every so often. "Phew. This walk didn't seem so long eighty-five years ago."

"What do you mean?"

"I grew up here, in Gray House. Lived here until, well, that doesn't matter so much." He paused, wheezing. "One moment, please."

He'd grown up here? Kelly tried to guess at his age. "What about the rest of your family?"

"Had a sister, who had a son. I married once, had a daughter. My wife died too young, when our daughter was barely a teenager. Something died inside me, too." He rolled along a few more feet, then paused again. "I'm one hundred two years old."

She'd never met anyone that old before. He was right, too. She brimmed with questions, but held herself back. She'd learn some answers when he spoke to the reporter, or so she hoped.

"We used to slide on the carpets that lined this hall, Tildie and me." Mr. Plummer continued on his way. "The banister also had plenty of polish, us sliding down when no one was looking."

"I—I like this old place." She almost blurted out about Mary Gray's diary, but didn't want that topic to trail into the interview. It felt almost like betraying a confidence.

"Has it shared any of its secrets with you?" He halted again, this time staring at her, his dark blue eyes watery yet probing.

"As a matter of fact, it has." She could tell him that much. "The first day I moved in."

"Ah, she has a lot of secrets. Happy ones, sad ones." Mr. Plummer sighed as they continued down the hallway. "I used to spend hours in the lookout at the top of the house. A great hiding place from nosy people. It was where I proposed to my sweetheart."

"I'm glad this house has had some happy memories," Kelly said. "It's had plenty of sad ones."

"What do you mean by that?"

Kelly glanced toward the ballroom. "I . . . I found Mary Gray's diary."

"Mary Gray's diary?" His voice rang out, louder than she expected. She tried not to cringe.

"Yes, I've been reading it." Which would probably stop, now that he was here.

"She was my great-grandmother." Mr. Plummer shook his head. "You would probably do well to not read it. She went insane not long after my grandfather was born."

"Insane?" The hair on Kelly's forearms prickled. Hiram Junior, little Hiram, was Mr. Plummer's grandfather? If Mr. Plummer was ninety-five now . . . she clicked back with the math. Hiram could have been sixty-one when Mr. Plummer was born.

"Best not talk about it now, not with the reporter here." Mr. Plummer tightened his grip on the rolling walker and continued his shuffle. "One thing I've learned, you don't have to share everything you know. Not until the right time, anyway."

"I see." She moved ahead of him to open the pocket door to the ballroom a little wider.

"Are you sure you see? I'll share this with you." He glanced toward Megan, who was typing on her phone, then back at Kelly. "Come closer."

She took a step so the rolling walker was the only thing between her and the elderly man, then leaned her head toward his.

"I know your secret, too," he whispered.

Kelly snapped upright, then forced herself to be still.

"You must be Mr. Plummer," Megan was saying as she crossed the ballroom, her right hand extended. "Thank you for coming today."

Somehow, Kelly found her way to the edge of the table closest to her. The quilt lay there, as if waiting for her to sit down and work on it.

*I know your secret, too.* What could he mean by that? He knew about Peyton and the museum disaster that nearly tanked her career? She couldn't think of anything else she'd like to bury about herself. Lots of people had families who were losers. They usually didn't end up in foster care, but it seemed most families had elements of dysfunction. So it couldn't be that.

She wanted to talk to Tom, but he'd been scarce lately, especially after the night at the waterfront. They'd inched closer to each other, literally and figuratively speaking, and the quick kiss had been an impulse of the moment that had paid her back with a few sleepless nights. But now she wanted nothing more than to talk to him about the odd Mr. Plummer.

The old man even now was making a sweep around the room with his rolling walker, Megan nodding and taking notes in his wake.

"Ah, the parties we would have here. One time, I even rode my horse through the room. There are double doors, or were, that opened onto a patio that overlooks the gardens." At that comment, Kelly fixed her attention back on Mr. Plummer.

"Which is why I hired someone to get the grounds back in shape. This is a big place that needs lots of nurturing, or TLC as the younger ones would say."

"Do you want to talk to Ms. Frost about the quilt before we leave the room?"

"Of course I do." He shuffled back in Kelly's direction, who braced herself.

"Look at this. Look at what you've done." Mr. Plummer was shaking his head. "I can see it from when I was a youngster. Never could get rid of the smoke smell. When I was little, my mother tried to clean it, but stopped because it started falling apart."

"It's quite fragile," Kelly agreed. "I've hesitated to do too much to it because I don't want to weaken it further. I've used vintage fabrics to replace some of the missing or frayed compass pieces. Not an ideal fix, but it works, I think."

"When the house opens officially, I want this to be on display on one of the beds. Perhaps the guest bed. Or the lady's bedroom." Mr. Plummer tapped the table. "Ms. Frost, you have done excellent work, and I will be happy to refer you to anyplace you'd like to go. Except, maybe there are other pieces in this house that could use your touch? Time is of the essence, as they say."

"I'm . . . I'm sure there are." Her mind flew back to the woven carpet in the drawing room.

"We can talk another time about future projects. But soon, soon."

She nodded and watched as the two of them left the ballroom. A chance to stay here, if she wanted? Maybe she could get her own apartment or studio, if Plummer would relax the on-site requirement. The man certainly seemed more approachable than Mr. Chandler.

Kelly went to the nearest window that overlooked the gardens. They flourished, the lawn a striking shade of emerald with Tom's care. Despite his reluctant gardener status, he was a natural.

She squinted out at the sunlit grounds. Was he there today? Surely he must be, with the reporter visiting. Megan also took her own photos as well. Kelly forced herself to stand naturally instead of freezing up in front of the camera.

Again, Mr. Plummer's words came back. *I know your secret, too.*

———

Free at last! Tom felt the wind rush past him on his motorcycle. MRI—scheduled early—clear. Neurologist gave him the news yesterday, and adjusted his medications. *Thank you, God. Thank you.*

His bank account was aided by the check that Dave Winthrop had given him after finishing the flooring and tile job at the townhouse. He would take the positive approach and count his blessings, one by one.

This was one of the few times since waking up in a hospital in Kuwait that he'd felt that glimmer of hope. He was on track again, even if he wasn't exactly sure where the track was taking him. Pop and the whole genealogy records from Winthrop helped too. Sometimes looking back helped nudge you forward, even just a little.

And the other night, jazz at the waterfront with Kelly. Nights like that he'd like to record so he could watch over and over. He and Kelly had both let some of their guard down and realized they'd found common ground between them.

Her project was more than two-thirds complete, and after that, there was nothing to tie her to New Bedford. Part of him wanted to ask her to stay, to see what else happened between them. Whatever it was, it was brand-new, sweet as the simple kiss she'd given him.

But part of him still held back. Self-preservation had taught him to be careful. Maybe it was part of his suspicious nature that he still had to deal with, or maybe there was something to it. Chandler had asked him to keep an eye on Kelly. Tom thought it ludicrous, but still.

What if there was something about Kelly he'd rather not know, that he'd discover? She knew most of his dirty laundry, thanks to his family's intervention in their friendship that had morphed into . . . well, he wasn't sure what.

Tom shoved thoughts of Kelly aside for the moment as he zipped along the streets in the direction of County Street and its rows of nineteenth-century homes. Owning something like that was out of his budget, but he did know one day he wanted to own something with history, something he could fix up and customize yet keep some of the original character.

One day this, one day that. He pulled into the rear entrance to the Gray House property after passing a pair of vehicles parked out front at the curb. Visitors?

Then he wanted to slap his forehead after parking his motorcycle. The reporter. Plus someone from Firstborn Holdings. Not Chandler this time, who'd contacted Tom about the interview date. He didn't sound too happy about the event, but nothing that uptight lawyer could do about it.

This all meant he needed to be prepared to show off the grounds. The automatic sprinklers he'd installed had left sparkling water drops across the lawn. Nice touch. The rosebushes were clipped a tad short, but there had been years of old dead growth left on them. The greenhouse was full of herbs and vegetables, with a few orchids he was coaxing to grow.

He'd signed up for a class at the community college, a local horticulture class, that would start sometime in late August. He wanted to learn more. There was little to risk by taking the non-credit class, but everything to gain.

He parked the motorcycle and removed his helmet. The back door opened and an unfamiliar woman emerged first. She turned to help an elderly man across the covered porch, then down the wide steps. Kelly followed, carrying a rolling walker.

Weak in body, the man rolled his way across to the motor-cycle. "Jonas Plummer. You must be Thomas Pereira."

"I am." He shot Kelly a questioning look, and she nodded.

"I'm CEO of Firstborn Holdings, and I'm taking these pretty ladies on a tour of my home."

"Your home. I thought . . ."

"You thought a company owned it. Of course it does. My company. It's too impractical to live here." Jonas Plummer took a slow glance over his shoulder at the house. "But recent devel-opments in my personal circumstances have made me see that I should tend to this, for my family's sake."

"I can understand that." Tom shook hands with the man. His fingers felt soft, but there was a wiry strength inside them. "How about I show you the gardens, then?"

"I'm up for it." But Jonas wheezed. "So long as I take my time, of course."

"You'll see I've reseeded and fertilized. Chandler, I mean Mr. Chandler, gave me strict instructions to make sure the lawn is mowed once a week."

Jonas said nothing, but kept rolling his walker, its wheels clicking on the cobbled pathway. He grunted when one wheel stuck in a crack where some of the filler between the cobbles had crumbled away.

"Need to fix these pathways. Find yourself a stone worker. Send me the estimate."

"All right." He glanced toward the women, who still stood by the steps, talking.

"Never mind them. A pretty lady can be a distraction, you know."

How well he knew. "You've got that right."

"It looks good, Son. Really good."

The other woman, not Kelly as he'd hoped, joined them on the path. "Tom, I'm Megan Hughes with the *New Bedford Star*. I'm writing an article on the comeback of Gray House."

"That's what I heard."

"If you could tell me what you've worked on since coming here and share about your future plans for the property." She licked her lips and paused, the tip of her pen in the air.

"I first started with snow removal, then was hired for lawn maintenance and gardening," said Tom.

"What was your background before working here?"

"I was in the United States Army, went through three tours in Southwest Asia before getting injured and medically discharged." The words sounded practiced. It seemed as if that entire segment of his life had been lived out by someone else. His old self, maybe, with his new self still growing accustomed to his new reality.

"Thank you for serving our country, Mr. Pereira." Jonas extended his hand once again, which Tom shook. "I was once First Lieutenant Jonas Plummer, United States Air Force, 1941 through 1948. The worst days of my life and the best days."

"I wanted to stay, Mr. Plummer." They reached the greenhouse.

But it was Megan who answered. "So you're working here now. Did you know you're not alone? A lot of veterans have found themselves out of work after entering the civilian world once again."

"I'm not surprised." Tom pushed open the greenhouse door. "Anyway, we have some herbs started here and some vegetables. I'm not sure what we can do with them all. Maybe there's a food pantry or shelter that could use them?"

"That's a good idea," Jonas said. "It's about time Gray House starts doing something good for someone."

Megan scribbled wildly on her notepad. Tom nodded.

"You two are so very young. I've got a heap of regrets that only now I've started making restitution for. God knows it will never be enough, but selfishness tends to run in my family, it seems. We only see what we want and can't imagine the rest of the world not bowing to our wishes." He turned himself around and plopped onto the seat of his rolling walker. "Get Tara for me. The interview's done."

"Who's Tara?" Tom asked.

"She drove him here," Megan explained. "She's in the house. I'll let her know that Mr. Plummer is ready to leave." She scurried back across the expanse of lawn to the house.

Tom almost chuckled at Jonas's actions. Definitely in charge and making sure everyone did as he told, but still seeing the need to make up for any selfishness on his part. He wished all along that Mr. Plummer had come to see them instead of having to deal with someone like Chandler.

"Mr. Plummer, can I get you some ice water or something? It's a humid day today."

"No, I'm fine. Glad I got that pretty little hovering thing away from us, though." Jonas sighed. "Maybe my lawyer was right. Maybe this wasn't a good idea."

"What do you mean, the article?"

"That's exactly what I mean." Jonas frowned. "But it's important. It's important I set things right for everyone while I have the chance, especially her."

"Especially who?" Tom had no idea what the man was getting at.

"Never mind." Jonas looked at him with sad eyes. "Thank you for helping take good care of my house."

# 15

*October 1852*

*Hiram is home. Esteban has gone, taking Peter with him. I ache inside, but it must be this way until I can tell Hiram once and for all how things will be between us. I am going to leave him. Hiram suspects nothing, but demands everything upon his return. He comes to me his first night home, and he repulses me. I know without asking him that he has satisfied himself with another woman's embrace, despite his pious manner. Yet I am the one who is a scarlet woman, and he the great ship's captain. I try to comfort myself by tending to little Hiram, but he pulls away from me and instead runs to his papa.*

*I try to tell Hiram that I do not love him, that I will leave him as soon as arrangements can be made. He laughs at me. I try to explain that there is someone else.*

*"You have admitted your sinful ways to me, yet you expect me to let you go?"*

*His response was to lock me in my rooms for two weeks, with only bread and water.*

*I have missed my agreed-upon meeting time with Esteban. My heart aches to be with him and with our little Peter.*

Not a good way to start the morning. Kelly's heart ached for Mary. In Mary's mind, it seemed that she would get her way. She probably hadn't counted on Hiram Gray's pride that made him keep his wife in submission at any costs. And poor Peter, without his mother. Surely the Delgados were good people, but then, she didn't know much about Esteban, other than he was a carpenter and didn't respect Mary's marital status. Kelly tried not to sigh. These people were long gone, their stories told and ended, and all that remained was a house, a journal, and a quilt.

Jonas Plummer's warning rang in Kelly's ears as she set the journal down, that no good could come of reading it. She'd wanted to ask him that day he toured Gray House if he'd read it as well, and what he knew of Mary Gray.

That never happened. She'd tried calling his office at Firstborn Holdings, but never received a response. Likely he didn't go to the office, given his health. Or maybe somehow Mr. Chandler had soured him against her.

She took a sip of her morning coffee. It was her day to call Lottie before she got too busy, so she started dialing before the day's work carried her away.

"How's my girl?" Lottie asked on answering the phone.

"Terrific, I think."

"Terrific? You just think, though."

"Things are going well. I met the real owner of Gray House, and he's happy with my work. I have a feeling he might hire me to do more."

"Oh, praise the Lord! I've been praying for you, dear, that you'd find something else after this." But her voice sounded a little sad.

"What is it, Lottie?"

"I wish you'd come visit me, even for a few days. I know you're working there, but surely you can take some time off."

"You know, that sounds like a good idea. But actually, I'll be through with the quilt before too long. Maybe I can take a week or so and visit then, instead of a few days." Then Kelly had another thought. "Or, you could come here. We could do the tourist thing and see the museums."

"That does sound fun."

"You can see the quilt firsthand, too. I would even let you copy the pattern to use yourself, if you wanted."

"Ah, now I am tempted for sure to close the store and drive down. Did you know, I've never seen your work? Not counting pieces you've created from scratch, of course."

"I didn't know that."

"I would love to see your work. I'm proud of you."

"Thank you, Lottie. That means a lot." She thought for a moment. "Oh, when you come for a visit, you can meet Tom."

"Tom, huh? You've mentioned him quite a few times."

Kelly's cheeks flushed. "Yes, he's . . . he's different from any-one I've ever known. And, well, he gets me, too. I don't think I've ever felt that with anyone else."

"Is he a believer?"

"Oh, yes, definitely. He's had some hard times, but he's coming through the other side."

"I can't wait to meet him."

"Good." Kelly crossed the kitchen and stopped at the back door. "The paper should be here now, too. Remember the article I told you about, how the reporter came and saw the quilt and toured the house? Well, that's come out today."

"Get me a copy, if you can."

"I will."

"Ah, I hear the busy tone coming into your voice. I'll let you go. Don't forget to call."

"I won't."

Kelly ran outside for the paper, then back in. She paged through to the "Living" section and found the story. Three photos, one of the house, another of Tom talking to Mr. Plummer at the garden, and the third of her with the quilt. She was saying something, gesturing down at the fabric. She thought she was probably explaining the difficult choices she'd had to make to keep the quilt from disintegrating.

She read the article. Megan Hughes had done well, even giving Kelly some free advertising.

*While Frost isn't sure what's next on her professional schedule, she looks forward to doing what she's done for nearly a decade—bringing textiles back from the edge of ruin.*

Megan had made Tom sound brave and strong after his ordeals, and it was as if being at Gray House had brought both Kelly and Tom second chances at their crossroads in life.

Even with learning Mary Gray's sad tale, Kelly felt hope. If God was her heavenly father, surely He was charting her course on the open seas of life, guiding her on her voyage. The nautical analogy seemed to fit, especially after being buffeted by the storms of life.

She headed to the quilt again, as she had for many mornings. Her training taught her certain things—that she could never restore a piece without losing some of the original, for one thing. But this quilt was special. The old had mingled with the new.

Her phone warbled again, just as she'd pulled on her gloves to begin work.

Jonna. Someone must have been reading the paper.

"Hello, Jonna."

"I see you've worked your new little angle to your advantage."

"Nice to talk to you, too. I never asked to be interviewed. I've been busy here."

"So have I."

"You're calling me because . . . ?" Kelly tried to think of why. "The dirt's already been slung, you know. You've won. You got the higher-paying job. You've probably got work lined up for a year or two out. FYI, I only have work for the next two weeks or so, maybe three."

"Uh, um . . ."

"People already know about Peyton and me. Why do you think my work in Boston has fizzled?" Amazing, now that the truth was out. She'd beaten herself up over it, but now that she had nothing to hide, Jonna had no ammo.

"It just looks to me like you're trying anything for publicity."

"Don't worry about me. I'll figure something out. I think if you were in my position, you'd welcome the free exposure."

"True, but . . ."

"I don't think we have anything more to say to each other, then. I wish you the best on your project." With that, Kelly hung up. But her hands were shaking.

Before, she'd let Jonna get to her. But now, she realized Jonna could do nothing to her that hadn't already happened. Yes, she and Peyton had been wrong. But that was past. Firmly in the past. *Thank You, God, for holding my future, even when I can't see it.*

⌒⌒⌒

Sunday supper at his parents' house. Tom found the scene idyllic, with all of them around the table. All of them and Kelly. She filled a good spot, joking with Hunter and Hailey, chatting about Europe with Bella. Of course Angela liked her. The two were already making plans to go shopping at the outlets in Fall River one day.

"So you're almost finished with the quilt, then?" his mother asked Kelly as they were clearing the table for a rousing game of dominoes.

"Almost." Kelly's glance bounced off him.

"What are you going to do after that?"

"I'm not sure yet. Mr. Plummer, that's the CEO, had mentioned once about some other projects in the house that need some conservation, but I haven't heard anything more." She stacked a few of the dirty plates.

"Oh, hon, don't worry about the plates and such. We'll take care of them." Tom's mother took the plates from Kelly's hands. "Well, I sure hope you'll find a way to stay around here."

Tom had a flashback to the first time she'd come to supper after his seizure. "I'm sure she'll go where she has work."

"I'd . . . I'd like to stay in the area, if it works out," Kelly said. "It's really grown on me."

"Well, we hope you stay. Don't we, Tom?"

"Of course we do."

Kelly giggled at his discomfort. Funny, she thought it was amusing when he was in the hot seat.

"You're famous now, Uncle Tom," said Hunter. "You had your picture in the paper."

"Not quite famous," Tom said, tousling Hunter's mop of hair. Thank goodness somebody changed the subject. "One day I'm sure you'll get your picture in the paper, too."

"Then I'll be famous." Hunter pointed at his chest.

"You are a little famous," said Kelly. "Didn't you tell me you've had several calls for work since the article ran? Plus someone with the Wounded Warrior Transition program wants you to speak to a veterans' group about your story?"

"Really?" His father looked up from the Sunday paper. "That's good. That's very good."

"Kelly's right." Tom nodded. "I told them I don't mind sharing my story with them. I don't know how it'll help, but I figured, why not? If what I've been through can help someone, I should give it a try." Talk about being in the hot seat. But Kelly beamed at him, the same look of pride he saw with his mother.

"We're proud of you, Son," his father said.

"Thanks, Pop." Today he wasn't expecting to get choked up. All this was supposed to be was a simple family dinner after Sunday church service. He'd invited Kelly to his church, which she liked better than the other she'd been visiting since living in New Bedford. Part of him wanted to believe it was because of him.

But now was one of "those" moments when you looked back at it, and you knew everything had changed. He wanted Kelly to be part of his life. The idea of her leaving . . . Yet she said she was open to staying.

Her phone rang, and she glanced at it. "Excuse me. Sorry about that." She left the dining room and went to the living room. He didn't miss the frown that clouded her face.

"She's the proverbial keeper, Tom." His mother beamed. "You definitely have our blessing."

"Ma, it's a little early for that." He tried not to sputter. "Hold your proverbial horses."

"I'm just telling you."

"Honey, let the man breathe," his pop spoke up from the end of the table.

Kelly reentered the dining room. "I'm not feeling very well. Do you mind taking me back to the house?"

"Of course not," Tom began.

"You're welcome to lie down here in our spare room," said Mom. "The thought of you in that big old house by yourself. Maybe you'll feel better a little later."

"Well, I don't know."

Tom stepped closer to her. "What's wrong?" She wasn't telling him something. Her face had a walled-in expression.

She glanced at his mother. "Thanks, maybe I just need to lie down for a while."

"This heat wave plus the humidity can't be good for anybody," Mom said. "Is there air conditioning in that big old place?"

"I have a window unit for my room, plus another portable one for the ballroom."

"That's ridiculous." She shook her head. "Tom, get her a fresh blanket and a pillow for the guest room."

"I don't think she'll need a blanket."

Kelly laid her hand on his arm. "That's fine."

He led her from the dining room. "C'mon, I'll show you where the guest room is." She followed him upstairs, stairs he'd pounded up and down countless times. The stairs gave their familiar creak.

"So," he said as he opened the door of the linen closet, "here's a blanket. It might be ninety degrees out, but Mom wants you to feel cozy."

"Thanks."

He took her to the second room on the right, past Bella's door. Giggles came from inside the room. He thought about telling Bella to keep it down, but then, she'd said something about heading out with some friends soon.

"And here's the guest room." Tom flung open the door. "It used to be mine."

"Ah, okay." She entered ahead of him and put the blanket on the bed. He held a pillow out to her, which she accepted.

"Kelly, what's wrong?" He put his hand on her shoulder.

"I don't feel like talking about it right now." She shrugged, then frowned. "I'll . . . I'll tell you. I promise. I just need a few minutes. Please."

"Okay." He pulled her into his arms and she leaned against him. "Take some time. We'll be downstairs. I'll be here."

"Thanks."

---

Peyton Greaves had called. She knew the number, although she'd deleted it from her phone. Months and months had gone by. Seeing the number made her stomach quiver. She knew enough if she didn't answer his call right there in the Pereiras' living room, he'd keep calling. The man had the gift of persistence. He'd used it successfully on her numerous times in the past.

He missed her, he said. He found out about the article and thought it was great. She kept her composure, but her hands shook when she pushed the end button on her phone.

Her first inclination was to run, hide, barricade herself literally and figuratively in the big old house. No, she wasn't about to go back to him. She wasn't about to now.

For now, though, she'd give herself some space in the comfort of Tom's old bedroom, now the official guest room for the Pereira family. She found herself searching the walls for some photo of Tom or a memento of his childhood. Nothing.

Kelly sank onto the twin bed tucked under a lone window. She could take a few minutes, then pull herself together and rejoin them.

She placed the pillow at the head of the bed, then kicked off her shoes. A rest couldn't hurt anything. Or call it a timeout. Kelly lay back onto the bedspread and studied the ceiling.

---

Today, the old man was sitting up in bed and wearing a jacket that would make Hugh Hefner turn green as Kermit the frog.

"I'm not going to offer you my opinion anymore," he told the old man. "You're just going to do what you want to do anyway."

"Of course I am."

He hadn't seen the old man this spry in forever. "You're not thinking clearly. I should call your doctor and see about upping or adjusting your medication."

"Keep talking like that and I'll fire you."

"You can't let me go." He tried not to sound panicked, but there it was, the tone in his voice that sure enough probably let the old man know he had him cornered.

"You're fired. Leave now before I get security involved." The old man glared at him. "I'm not joking."

"You're making a big mistake. Just watch and see."

"Is that a threat?"

He stopped in the doorway just before he left. "I'm not joking, either."

# 16

March 1853

*Hiram is setting sail once more. I sent word to Esteban through his sister, the seamstress, who helped me begin the quilt. I tell him that I am ready to work on his reading lessons once again. Esteban does not come to our customary spot. My desolation gives me a physical ache. I decided to disguise myself and take a cab to his section of town. There is Esteban, walking the cobblestoned streets with a dark-haired beauty. I find his mother's house and she turns me away, screaming at me in Portuguese. I know enough to discern that I have lost my little Peter forever.*

Unbelievable. Kelly could scarcely breathe as she read the section of diary. Betrayed again, poor Mary. She shook her head. All of Mary's plans and dreams had crumbled, although she had relief with Hiram heading to sea again.

Little Peter, never knowing his true mother. Did Esteban ever take him aside as he grew older and tell him of his parentage? With every new element of Mary's story coming to light, yet another question arose as well.

Maybe some questions were meant to stay unanswered.

She reminded herself of the lovely evening she knew lay ahead. She and Tom were going to have supper together. He had brought a grill to Gray House, and she had steaks marinating in the fridge downstairs. He promised her jazz with supper, and she promised she would make dessert. Out of a box, but it was still chocolate mousse.

She wasn't sure if she ought to dress up or anything, but thought comfort would be the best way to go. Not her usual work attire, but a cotton peasant blouse with fresh capris would be fine. Tonight promised a full moon, too.

*Lord, I can't remember the last time I was this happy.*

The phone had remained silent as far as Peyton was concerned, too.

At last, the shadows were long and the sun was headed toward the western horizon. Kelly was rummaging in the refrigerator when a knock sounded at the back door.

She flung the door open. "Tom."

He stood there, grinning, and her heartbeat ramped up just a little. "The grill's lit, should be ready for steaks soon."

"Good. I've been looking forward to this all day."

"Me too."

She managed to shove her worries aside for the next two hours, and told Tom so. "I have a hard time enjoying myself when things go right," she admitted as they watched the last red glow in the west disappear.

"Why's that?" he asked. They sat on the porch steps, leaning comfortably on each other.

"I'm waiting for the other shoe to drop, so to speak. That good times never last. And I don't like feeling that way. It's not like I'm expecting life to go my way all the time. I know that's impossible. But it's hard to enjoy myself when things do go right." The admission almost sounded foolish, now that she said it aloud.

"I understand what you mean." A soft breeze gave relief from the heat of the day.

"I'm glad you do."

"Hey, I want to show you something." He reached for her hand, then stood, pulling her to her feet. "I wasn't sure if it would work, but it has."

Now that the moon had made its appearance, it gave a glow to the cobblestones that wound through the property. Kelly didn't need to worry about her footing, not when she was floating beside Tom, his hand holding hers.

"It's the heirloom rosebush," Tom announced as they reached a remote corner of the garden. "I've been working on it all summer, trying to get it to take hold. And now look."

Kelly stepped closer to the little plant, barely two feet tall. A single bud bloomed on the uppermost branch. "Oh, wow."

"I was told this came from an original cutting over one hundred years ago."

She leaned closer to smell it. Not much, maybe a whiff of rose. But it was something.

"Kelly."

She straightened and faced Tom.

It was the most natural thing in the world to surrender to the circle of his arms and let him kiss her, not like the quick kiss at the harbor. She could stay like this and skip the dessert that they hadn't eaten yet.

The kiss ended, a little soon for her liking, but it was probably a good idea that it did. She rested her head on his chest and listened to his heartbeat, galloping away just like hers was.

"I've wanted to do that for a long time," he said.

"I'm glad you did." He worked out, and she could tell.

Then she blinked at the annoying glare of headlights. Who in the world? There had better be a good reason for someone to show up at the house, this time of night. She pulled away from Tom and stared across the lawn at the vehicle.

The headlights dimmed and a car door opened. "Kelly, is that you over there?"

She squinted toward the figure. Her spine stiffened. No way. Not here.

"Peyton?"

"I came to see you, in person, because I had to."

"No, you didn't." She started marching along the cobble-stones in Peyton's direction.

"Kelly, what's this all about?" Tom asked as he walked beside her.

"Nothing. Nothing at all." She stopped a few feet from Peyton's car. He'd driven two hours to see her, straight from the office it looked like, judging by his loosened tie.

"I had to see you," Peyton repeated. "These last six months have been torture for me."

"Peyton, you have a *wife*, if you've forgotten. You definitely forgot to mention her to me." She couldn't bear to look at Tom, now that their perfect evening was in ruins.

"Not for long. She kicked me out in April. I've . . . I got my own place now. The divorce . . ." Peyton sighed and leaned against his car. "The divorce will be final tomorrow."

"I'm sorry that happened," Kelly said. She was sorry, for sure. "I'm sorry for my part in that." Even worse, she was sorry Tom was witnessing this, firsthand. What he must think of her now . . .

"But don't you see? I'm free now."

"Excuse me for interrupting, but you've upset Kelly. I think you need to leave." Tom stepped forward.

"I'll do no such thing." Peyton stepped forward as well. "Kelly and I have a relationship that goes back farther than anything she thinks she has here with you."

"Stop it." Kelly moved closer to Peyton. "We're over. We were over in January. In case you forgot, it affected my career.

You think I'm going to get another contract with anyone attached to the BFA? Especially anyone who knows your wife, or ex-wife?"

"That's getting to be old news. I knew it would, eventually."

Kelly shook her head. "How can you say that? It's hounded me for months. I'm thankful this job turned up for me here."

"New job, new boyfriend, is that what it is?" Peyton shot a glare at Tom. "I'll tell you this. I taught her most of what she knows."

"How dare you—" Kelly marched up to Peyton. He yanked her to him and started kissing her.

All the memories came rushing back, and her mind went numb. For a few seconds, she almost wanted Peyton back again.

*Tom.*

She jerked away from Peyton, bumping into Tom as she did so.

Tom shoved Peyton onto the hood of the car, then stopped. "Leave now. Don't you ever come back. If I see you on this property again, I'm calling the police. Don't call her, either."

Peyton glanced from her to Tom, then back at her again. "Fine. If you thought you had a hard time getting work now, you don't want to see what it'll be like from now on."

He left, tires shrieking on the pavement.

Kelly's hands shook, too. The woman caught in adultery, who the Pharisees flung before Jesus, demanding judgment? Yep, she knew the feeling. No matter that the guy was now heading back to Boston. She couldn't even look at Tom.

"The guy was *married*?" he asked, breathing hard.

"Yes. He . . . he never told me. I found out the hard way. Then I broke up with him. Someone found out about us, and it was a big mess." She wanted to explain that she wasn't that woman anymore, but couldn't find the words. And after what Peyton said about her . . .

"I think I'm going home now." Tom's voice was flat.

"Tom, can I explain?"

"I don't know. Maybe. But not right now." He took a few steps away from her and toward his motorcycle. "Good night."

She wanted to beg him to stay, to listen. He'd stuck up for her. But then, Tom Pereira was that kind of man. *God, please, how long must I keep paying for my sins of the past?*

———

What was the old saying about a sucker being born every minute?

Tom sat up that night, insomnia his old friend back again. He typed the name Peyton and Boston Fine Arts Museum into the Internet search engine. Up popped plenty of links. Old photos.

The guy was some bigwig administrator, director of gallery programs. There were a few photos of him with Kelly and a few others. Kelly, in a magnificent little black dress. No wonder Peyton had fallen for her. She looked exquisite with the contrast made by her creamy skin, light blue eyes, and silken hair.

He'd fallen for that, too, with no little black dress involved.

Reading between the lines, he saw Kelly's close relationship with the museum and then with Peyton. Hidden in plain sight, their relationship was risky. How could Kelly not have known? That was a stretch for Tom. Either she'd been super naïve or willfully ignored Peyton's marital state.

Tom had been ready to plaster the guy against the car and then some. He'd made Kelly out to be some kind of tawdry woman under his tutelage. It cheapened the sweet yet passionate kiss they'd shared in the garden mere moments before Peyton roared onto the scene.

The anger that roared up inside frightened him, and now a headache made him feel as if a giant's vise were tightening around his head. Not good.

Then came the detached feeling of a seizure. He had his parents on speed dial. "Mom . . ."

His last conscious thought was gratefulness that it didn't happen in front of Kelly or Pretty Boy Peyton from the museum.

# 17

*April 1853*

*They say a madwoman cannot make sense of the world around her, let alone write about it, but I can. My empty arms are now full, but my heart tells me that it will never be full again. The one light of my life is gone from me, and I have no embers from which to coax a new spark.*

*My atonement is futile. I have no other choice than the one before me. If Almighty God is listening from Heaven, surely He will accept this sacrifice. Perhaps the generations to follow will as well.*

*I will pay for my sins by fire. We all return to ashes and dust. If it is my time now, then it is now.*

Kelly turned the page. There was nothing more in the journal. She closed the book and wiped her eyes. She'd had enough of Mary Gray's story, anyway. It was like watching a car accident. She knew what was going to happen, didn't want to watch, yet at the same time couldn't drag her attention away from the scene unfolding in front of her.

Poor, poor Mary.

Her own heart hurt. She'd wavered about Peyton for those few seconds, and that wasn't fair to Tom. It wasn't the truth. Peyton might have said his wife kicked him out in the spring, but that still didn't pave the way for them to be together. He'd sauntered into the garden, thinking she would run to his arms straightaway. No, she wasn't the same person she was last winter.

God had forgiven her, but that didn't mean she should walk right back into a relationship with a cheater. Cheaters knew how to cheat. If he cheated on his wife, who else would he cheat with? Probably her, too, if the right woman and circumstances presented themselves. Some people were like that. But not her. And then, there were the horrible things he'd said about her.

Tom had not shown up for work in several days. She had called him once, and it went straight to his voice mail. She told him she was sorry, and she wondered when he was coming back to work.

She stood and stretched. Mary's story had ended. The paper trail about a fire at Gray House had pointed to the mid-1850s, in an edition of the *New Bedford Journal*. The house was rebuilt, restored. A family eventually grew up inside its walls. Jonas Plummer had, for one thing. So the house never really changed hands, except on paper, to Plummer's company.

This was why she was here, to restore Mary's quilt or at least rescue it from disintegrating. Her own stitches had been full of hope that, yes, this treasure would remain to tell its story. It was a story of a sad, difficult life, stitched with joy and trimmed with sorrow. Much of Mary's heartache had been from her own choices.

With this final journal entry, Kelly wanted to pick up a pen and write another ending, that Captain Gray and Mary had renewed their love for each other, that she had more children to raise along with little Hiram. Not that any of them would replace her Peter, but that Mary would continue to live a full life in spite of herself. She hadn't chosen to marry into a one-sided marriage. The long separations had been difficult on Mary.

She wanted to rewrite her own story as well, especially what had happened the other night.

Kelly stood and stretched, wincing as her shoulder tightened up again. She had slacked off on her exercises in an effort to get the quilt finished. Stitch by stitch, hour by hour, day by day, she'd worked her way along the points of the compasses covering the quilt top. Only the backing and binding remained now.

After what happened with Tom and Peyton, she couldn't be finished soon enough. Part of her wanted to call Tom, to beg him to understand that she was through with Peyton, that his charms didn't work on her. Of course, she wasn't immune to them. A woman couldn't help but find him charming. But charming didn't mean a man was honorable. Charming no longer meant she'd crumbled, now that her eyes were opened.

Tom had never lied to her or pretended to be anyone other than who he was. And she loved him for it. Seeing the hurt in his eyes in the garden, though, cut into her soul.

*Oh, God, forgive me for hurting him. I should have said something then, when Peyton called me after he read the article. I never expected Peyton to show up like that.* She sighed and stopped at the fireplace mantel. Maybe it would be better to stay in another room of the house, or better yet, find an inexpensive hotel to stay in until the project was done.

This was a sad house, and now that its secrets had been unloaded on her, she felt weary with the knowledge. Adding that to the fiasco with Tom and she was more than ready to be done with Gray House, New Bedford, and all reminders of her time here.

One good thing, she realized the family she had in Lottie. Her only regret was pushing Chuck and Lottie away for so many years during her youthful craving for independence.

The quilt waited for her downstairs. If she ignored the ache returning to her shoulder, she could finish within the next week. She had all she needed. The only thing that would make her needle move slower was the thought of leaving. But leaving as soon as the quilt was finished would be best. Maybe, just maybe, she'd get another commission because of the news reports about Gray House.

Kelly quickened her steps to the ballroom. Time to make an end of the quilt and be done with New Bedford.

---

*Stupid, stupid, stupid.* He should have known better. When that Peyton guy showed up at the house, whatever Tom thought he had—or might have had—with Kelly splintered into a million jagged pieces and blew away, straight at him. He'd seen the wavering in her eyes, for just a millisecond, but it was there.

And he'd been foolish enough to hope that somehow he could persuade her to stay in New Bedford, to give their relationship a chance. His family couldn't stop talking about her and had all but given her their stamp of approval.

He'd walked right into this. Tom paced his apartment, not allowing himself to punch a wall. Expensive mistakes in the heat of anger were never smart. He stomped to the front window and looked out at the rooftops of the other houses below his third-floor walk-up.

He'd spent a day in the hospital with yet another inconclusive MRI and a worried mother whom he wouldn't tell what was wrong.

*God, why?*

He told himself long ago he'd never ask that question again. Not after his injuries and medical discharge from the military, not when watching others achieve what he hadn't. Stable career. Someone to share his life with. A family. He liked his independence, but the more he'd spent time with Kelly, the more he couldn't imagine himself not having her in his life.

His phone buzzed on the kitchen island. Tom stomped over to it. He wasn't in the mood to talk and had half a mind to ignore the call. Angela. She never called. Something was up.

"Hey, Angie."

"Tom, I was supposed to meet up with Kelly to go to the outlet mall but she called and canceled. She sounded awful, told me she had a headache and maybe we could meet another time. What's really the story? I could tell she'd been crying."

"I don't want to talk about it."

"So something did happen with you two. What did you do?" Her tone was teasing, but the words nipped at him.

"It wasn't me." He rubbed his forehead. "Like I said, I don't want to talk about it."

"Well, I think you two should."

"Maybe we will. That ball's firmly in her court."

"Don't be so stubborn."

"Stubborn, nothing." It was called self-preservation. At least his mother hadn't called, seeking an update.

"Okay, I'll let you go. But brother-in-law of mine, don't let her go. She's one of a kind."

"Yes, she certainly is." He ended the call, then turned his phone off. He wasn't letting her go, not technically. Maybe just taking a step back until she figured out what she really wanted.

Kelly, having an affair with a married man. Tom tried to shake the idea from his mind. Yes, he could see a woman falling for someone like Peyton from the museum. With that affected almost-British accent, charm, and polish, he didn't blame a woman. But that Peyton was married . . .

Her stammered explanation still echoed in his ears. *Tom, I didn't know. Please, believe me. I'd fallen for him before I knew.*

Yes, just like he'd fallen for her before he knew about Peyton. She'd stood there and said it was over, but her hesitation told him otherwise. He wanted to hop on his motorcycle and drive until he ran out of gas.

Friday night, the weekend ahead of him. Why not?

He'd been cooped up until the doctor had cleared him to drive, and it felt like he had hundreds of unridden miles to make up for. He grabbed his phone, keys, and made sure he had his credit card. Who knew how far he'd get in eight hours, but he'd sure find out.

Kelly hesitated once before heading up the Pereiras' sidewalk. She had to know something, anything about Tom.

Mrs. Pereira opened the door, just before Kelly turned away. "Kelly, come in."

"I'm not staying long. I would have called ahead of time, but—"

"Whatever has happened between you and my son, I'm praying that you two work it out. I've never seen him like this, not since he first came home. I've tried calling him tonight, but he won't answer his phone."

"Ah, I see." So it wasn't just her. Maybe all they needed was a little bit of time. Surely he'd come back, at least to work at Gray House. "He's missed work for a few days."

"He had a seizure the other night and the doctor put him on bed rest."

"Is he okay?"

Mrs. Pereira nodded. "He's okay. We'd invited him to supper tonight, but he never came. I have a feeling he's gone for a ride on his motorcycle."

"Do you know when he'll be back?"

"That's hard to say." Mrs. Pereira shrugged. "Be patient. He'll be back."

Kelly drove home to the dark house, realizing she'd forgotten to set the security alarm when she left. Or had she? She sighed as she crossed the kitchen. Just that morning she'd finished reading Mary's journal and had set it on the table.

The space was empty.

Kelly pounded up the stairs and switched on a light. The bureau top was empty as well. Plus the side table by the window. No, the last place she'd read the journal was in the kitchen, with a cup of coffee that morning.

Someone had stolen Mary's journal.

<hr>

The engine roared in Tom's ears as he made space between New Bedford and his motorcycle. Freedom to think, to not think. Maybe the more miles between him and New Bedford, the better. Night had fallen, but heat still radiated up from the asphalt highway. The white center line blipped past just left of the front tire.

How far to go tonight before stopping? The lanes of highway snaked southeast along the Connecticut coast and toward New York. He didn't want more lights, but peace and quiet, both inside and out. He didn't even tell anyone he'd gone.

He zipped along as the minutes crept by, passing around the Big Apple. The city that never slept wasn't for him tonight.

People joked about the New Jersey shore, but he knew he'd find some quiet there. He probably could have driven all the way to Delaware tonight without stopping, but thought better of the idea. The beginning of a headache pricked at his temples.

He took the Garden State Parkway until the exit for the beach. The lowered speed limit made his pace mimic a crawl. In the next town, a billboard promised a simple motor hotel with rooms "just blocks from the beach." Fine with him. He easily found the horseshoe shaped one-story structure with a small rectangular swimming pool. The place reminded him of a retro motor court from an old movie. One last room available, and Tom paid for it with cash.

The room, simply furnished with beach-themed rattan furniture, felt stuffy and closed in. Tom switched on the window A/C unit. A walk would help him keep the fidgets away while the room temperature cooled.

He locked the door behind him and headed onto the sidewalk in the direction of the surf's call. One of the many restaurants along the boardwalk was still open, this one with saxophone music drifting out the open doors. They'd rebuilt after last fall's hurricane that flooded the town.

Tom wished he could rebuild what was damaged with Kelly, but didn't know how.

Tom's stomach growled. He'd missed his evening dose of medicine and supper, too. Neither of those were good things, and his doctor's chiding reminded him to take care of himself. He stepped into the restaurant and found an empty table. An old man played the saxophone, accompanied by a pianist in the background.

A server stopped at his table. "Something to drink?"

"Just coffee. Black. And a burger and fries, if your kitchen is still open."

"It is. I'll get your coffee for you now." His server disappeared into the rear of the restaurant.

LYNETTE SOWELL

His restless itch had brought him here, but nothing had changed. Maybe just for tonight he could forget what had happened.

He took out the folder of genealogy, looking back at the highlighted names, all the way back to Delgado on his father's side. The handwritten notes said Peter Delgado, but the census read Pedro. Coincidence?

The names from Kelly's tales of the journal came back to him. Mary and Esteban had a child together that she'd passed along to Esteban. Now what kind of a mother would do that? His name was Peter, or Pedro. Delgado.

His father's great-great-grandfather? Yet there it was on the census, Pedro Delgado, eight years old, listed on the census for the first time. The names matched up, too. Esteban was there, only twenty-two, listed below his parents as a separate head of household with the occupation of carpenter. He hadn't noticed that before.

He didn't think he'd bother telling his parents about that just yet. Which meant he was related to Mary Gray. His first impulse was to tell Kelly. No. He wouldn't do it. Eventually, he would. He owed her that much of the story.

"Your coffee." The server set down a mug in front of him on the plastic tabletop. "I'll be back soon with your food."

"Thanks." It was a sticky late-August night, maybe too hot for coffee, but Tom didn't want anything stronger.

He took a sip and let the heat slide down his throat. Better. He leaned back in his chair and listened to the saxophone's call.

One day he'd have to stop running. From people, from memories, from regrets. From his fear. Truth be told, he was terrified of pulling himself out of the shambles and holding pattern he'd lived in. It was easier to push things off on his scars. And then there was Kelly.

He'd fallen for her despite his resolve to stay uninvolved, to not let anyone in. But here he was, hundreds of miles from home. That showed him he was more than involved. She'd wormed her way into his heart, without any effort on her part.

He sipped his coffee and closed his eyes. The saxophone's music fell silent, and he and the few people gathered in the restaurant applauded. Good stuff, such soulful music. He heard the joy and pain, even longing, in the melody.

Someone stopped at his table, and he opened his eyes.

"You dining alone?" asked the saxophone player, with skin as dark as the coffee Tom drank.

Tom nodded. "Just had to get out for a while, and found this place." It was the shortest of the explanations he could come up with.

"You mind if I join you for a few moments?"

"Not at all, Mister . . . ?"

"Thompson. Billie Ray Thompson, originally of Memphis, Tennessee."

"You're a long way from Tennessee," Tom said.

"You're a long way from home yourself." Billie Ray squinted at Tom's clothing. "You don't look dressed for the beach, either."

"Nah. I had some troubles at home and figured I'd leave them behind for a while."

"For a while, huh?" Billie Ray grinned. "You know they'll be waiting for you when you get back."

"Sometimes we need a breather."

"That we do, that we do. So, what are you running from?"

Tom shrugged. "There's this woman . . . "

"A woman, huh? Now this is worth sittin' down for." Billie Ray pulled up a spare chair. "Those ladies, they heap plenty o' troubles on us, don't they?"

"I should have seen it coming."

"She run around on you, is that it?"

"No, she hasn't."

"She spent your money?"

"No."

"Killed your dog?"

"Now, that's ridiculous." The corners of Tom's mouth twitched. "No, she wouldn't do that."

"So what's she done that's so bad, that made you come all the way to the shore?"

"She made me fall in love with her."

"Made you, did she?" Billie Ray looked up.

A server held a plate of burger and fries. "Thanks," Tom said, as she placed it in front of him. "Yes, made me."

"What's wrong with that? Everybody needs somebody."

"Maybe they don't."

"Of course you do. And if the good Lord has seen fit to send you somebody, you should walk into it."

"Is that so?"

"Yes. 'Cause I wish I had." Billie Ray sighed. "I waited too long. She got tired of waiting. I wanted to be one-hundred percent sure. I didn't want to make a mistake. I seen too many bad marriages."

"What's wrong with being one-hundred percent sure?"

"Because love doesn't always give us the best percentages. We gotta rely on us working to love and God working through us to love." Billie Ray smiled up at the server, who placed a glass of ice water in front of him.

"You don't say."

"No, I do say." Billie Ray glanced at his watch. "I've got about five more minutes."

"Thanks for sitting with me."

"Thanks for listening to me. Don't wait too long, my friend."

"I'll think about it" was all Tom could say.

# 18

Tom drove the lawnmower into the storage shed, then cut the engine. He'd finished the lawn, right at twilight. What twilight there was tonight, that is. Clouds were rolling in from the northwest, and a rumble of thunder punctuated the humid atmosphere. Late August and the sticky heat clung to him, just like his shirt.

His Friday night ride to the Jersey shore behind him, and Monday had come and gone, with plenty to do at Gray House.

He hadn't spoken to Kelly since that Peyton character had shown up. Finally, he'd found the right time to kiss her, to feel as if they were truly together. Her work on the quilt was drawing to a close, and she wasn't sure what would come next. Tom wasn't sure if he could ask her to stay, to set up a studio in New Bedford and keep working with her special touch on her fabrics. He didn't understand it all, but he knew he wanted her to stay.

Then Peyton, the jerk, came in and ruined everything. Kelly had wavered with Peyton's assurances that he was ready to go back to the way they were. Why couldn't women see through a player's big talk? A cheater would always cheat.

The images he'd seen online, of Boston parties and the museum crowd, had plenty of Peyton and Kelly. Then the photos of Peyton and his wife. What a mess. He'd seen the confusion written on Kelly's face, too.

"Give her a chance," Ma had said. "She's hurting and healing. But I can tell she cares for you more than she's ready to say."

"I don't know . . ." Chandler's warning rang in his ears. Yet how many times had people given him another chance, more than once?

Billie Ray's warning also came to him. *Don't wait too long.*

A car rolled up onto the parking slab. Chandler. Good timing, like a root canal.

The man exited the vehicle. It was the first time that Tom had ever seen him not wear a suit jacket and tie. He looked ready for a clambake at the Vineyard in his khakis and polo shirt.

"Chandler."

"Pereira."

"What brings you here today? The lawn's trimmed, the garden's weeded, and the roses are free of black spot." He tried to remind himself that this was his boss's representative, but he wasn't in the mood to play nice.

"Business. As always, business." Chandler gestured toward the greenhouse. "May I see your progress on the native plants?"

Tom nodded. It was sort of odd, the guy having more than a passing interest in the grounds at Gray House. "Right this way." His head throbbed, probably due to the humidity and changing barometric pressure with a storm coming.

"So, here's the turn-of-the-twentieth-century herbs that your boss wanted." Tom pointed at the row of terracotta planters. "Soon we'll have a collection that any cook one hundred years ago would love to use."

"Well done." Chandler shook his head. "I never would have thought you'd put up with this job for so long."

"Times are tough. A job's a job." Tom shrugged. "Plus, what can I say? The place has grown on me. No pun intended. I think there's life in the old gray house."

"I see." Chandler started walking the aisles of the greenhouse, surveying the plants.

Tom picked up his courage. Finishing the townhouse project had given him some courage. If he could do the floors, surely he could round up a couple of friends to help him work on the ancient roof of Gray House.

"Say, Chandler. I noticed that the roof needs repairs, possibly replacement altogether. I've already been part of several roofing projects this past spring." Tom paused, waiting to see what Chandler would say. He didn't particularly like the guy, but he knew he was the go-between for the head of the company.

Silence. Chandler was studying the roses, the more than one-hundred-year-old bush that Tom had been coaxing back to life. A solitary bud had appeared on one of the spindly branches. The same one he'd shown Kelly the other night had now started to open.

"Resilient, isn't it?" Chandler asked.

"Ah, the rosebush." Tom nodded. "It's taken all summer. But I think this original bush will be ready to introduce back to the garden soon."

"Nothing like the original, is there? Any new plant is a hybrid, an imposter." Chandler's voice held a detached tone.

"What are you getting at?" The guy's attitude was a bit freaky. They were just plants. The old plant was irreplaceable, but really . . .

"The old man thinks you deserve his birthright." Chandler was shaking his head. "After all I've done for him, and I'm part of the *legitimate* line. Legitimate is the key word here."

"What are you talking about?" How did Chandler learn about his illegitimate connection to Gray House through Mary Gray?

Chandler pulled out a leather-bound book.

"How'd you get that?" Tom demanded.

"It's none of your concern." Chandler shook the journal. "See? This tells the whole story. The old man wants to give it all to you and that—that cheating—"

"Cheating what?" Tom clenched his hands into fists. "You don't talk about Kelly that way."

Chandler spoke one word, and it was enough for Tom to rush at him, slamming him into the door frame. The journal flew from his hand and thudded onto the packed-dirt floor.

"I can see you're in denial about Kelly Frost's true character. Remember, I wanted you to keep an eye on her." Chandler wheezed. Tom resisted the urge to land a punch. Lightning flashed in the windows.

"I don't care. But you'll not talk like that about her again." Tom's head swam. Likely his blood pressure had just shot up. He grabbed his forehead.

"It doesn't matter what you tell me. I've got the true bloodline. Ironic, that Captain Gray's progeny has fallen so far." Thunder cracked through the clouds outside, as if agreeing with Chandler's rant.

"Chandler, you need to get some help, or something."

"Right. I'll press charges for you attacking me as well."

Tom froze. Chandler had a point. He'd been the one to lose his cool when Chandler made the comment about Kelly.

"I can sue you for that. Remember, I'm a lawyer." Chandler took a few steps forward. "Last I knew, it was illegal to slam a man against a door frame for insulting his girlfriend."

Tom turned to face away from Chandler. A whooshing noise came to his ears. Then a searing pain, and nothing.

---

The lightning flash pulled Kelly's focus from the quilt. *Two, three, four* . . . She'd never dropped the childhood habit of counting the seconds until the crack of thunder followed. The storm was close. Good. Anything to break the late summer heat wave and its accompanying humidity. If only the coming storm could wash away the wall between her and Tom.

Sure, he was back from wherever he'd gone. But he didn't share anything with her. She'd met Angela for coffee, who'd encouraged her to give Tom some time.

If he was going to be stubborn, fine. There was nothing she could do about it.

A knock sounded at the front door. Hopefully, it wasn't someone else asking for a tour of Gray House. The media attention had garnered some interest for her about future conservation work, but also had pulled up its share of nosy neighbors who wanted to see the old house and hear about the quilt firsthand.

She headed for the front hallway, then unlatched the front door. "Mr. Chandler."

"May I . . . may I come in?" He sounded friendlier than she'd ever seen him.

"Of course. This isn't my home." She stepped back, allowing him into the entryway.

"Do you have a few moments? I know you've been working on the quilt, but I wanted to say thank you, and apologize." He lowered his head, nodding at her.

"I'm about ready to stop for the evening, so, sure." She figured she'd do the courteous thing. "Would you like some lemonade or iced tea? Or coffee? I can make a fresh pot."

"Something cold to drink would be fine." He gestured for her to walk ahead of him. "I won't be but a few minutes."

Kelly led him to the kitchen. Maybe he'd realized what a jerk he'd been this summer. Or maybe someone at work had told him to be polite. Either way, she'd take it. She wouldn't be here much longer anyway.

"I've made some fresh iced tea. It should be cool right about now."

"That's fine with me." Chandler sat down at one of the four wooden chairs that stood in front of the breakfast table.

She was fighting to stay polite, but this time it wasn't hard. The guy was actually acting half human for a change. She took out a pair of glass tumblers, set them on the counter, then fished the iced tea out of the refrigerator and poured them each a glass.

"You seem quite comfortable in this kitchen."

An odd change of subject. She shrugged. "As comfortable as I can be, I guess." She was going to say something about not being much of a cook, but her cell phone ringing made her pause. "If you'll hold on a minute, I'll be right back."

She scurried down the hall toward the ballroom where she'd left her phone. Give the guy his cold drink, send him on his way after she heard whatever his apology contained. Many times she'd been on the giving end of an apology. If he was going to apologize, she'd listen to him.

*Private caller.* That could be anyone. She tucked her phone into her pocket and returned to the kitchen. "Sorry about that."

The grayness of twilight descended outside, so Kelly switched on the kitchen light.

"We've got quite a storm coming in, I imagine," said Chandler.

Kelly nodded. "I'm looking forward to a break from the heat."

"As we all are." Chandler took a sip of his tea.

She picked up her own glass and took a swallow. "So, you said you wanted to apologize?"

Chandler nodded. "I realize I've been unfair in my attitude toward you. I questioned your motives for coming here, to Gray House."

"I came because I needed the money." She took another drink. "This is really going to boost my career, especially with the press surrounding the quilt and the house. I'm thankful to you and your company for helping with that."

"I know that your time here is coming to an end, but I'll be happy to write a letter of recommendation in the future regarding your work."

"Thanks, I appreciate . . . that." Her head had suddenly developed a swimmy feeling, like the time she'd gotten dehydrated. She took another sip of tea. "I'm not sure what's wrong with me."

"You're nothing but a money-grabbing little minx. You think that Jonas Plummer will give you his inheritance, you who've never been a part of his life?"

"What are you talking about? Jonas Plummer?"

"Your mother's great-grandfather."

Her brain had turned to marshmallow and her limbs had grown weak, but this news snapped her to attention. "He's my family?" She licked her lips and took another swig of tea. Maybe she'd been dehydrated and didn't realize it.

A slow nod from Chandler. "He wants you to have all this, but you deserve none of it. You're garbage, just like your mother."

She blinked at Chandler. There were two of him now across the table in front of her. "You did something . . . to the tea . . ." The man was bonkers, crazy for Cocoa Puffs, talking about her family. She pulled out her phone, which he yanked from her weakened fingers.

His nod was the last clear thing she saw before she slumped over the table, her fingertips brushing the glass of tea. Spilling liquid, then shattering glass.

Kelly fought against the blackness. A pair of hands gripped her by the shoulders.

"Don't fight me. It's better this way." Chandler's voice came from the end of some kind of tunnel.

Or pit. She was trapped in a pit and couldn't move, couldn't talk. With the last shreds of her consciousness, she struggled against the encroaching oblivion.

"No," she managed to moan. "Let me go. I don't care about the house." But that was too close to a lie for her comfort.

"Don't fight me on this," Chandler said as he dragged her up the stairs.

Oblivion won.

# 19

Kelly's head swam. She woke to a flash of lightning in the window. What had happened? She was talking to William Chandler . . . who was insane. She tried to move her arms, then realized she'd been tied, hands and feet, to the bed. She caught a whiff of kerosene, heard the trickle of liquid into a container.

"No." She pulled at the bonds that held her wrists. A floorboard creaked and a flashlight clicked on.

William Chandler stood steps from the side of the bed, a flashlight illuminating the room. "You're not going to get any of this. Come around, thinking that Jonas Plummer is going to give you a handout. But I know all about you. You will never be worthy of this legacy."

"What are you talking about?" Kelly tugged at the bonds. "I'm only here to restore a quilt." She saw a glass lantern in his hands.

"Right. You and Tom Pereira are only here to do your jobs." Mr. Chandler shook his head. "You have no rights to what I've claimed my whole life. I'm the one who put up with the old man's ramblings as he's slipped closer to the grave. The cancer will take him before his heart will, I think. And then I'm

189

ready. Ready for all of it." He set the lantern on the bureau next to Mary Gray's priceless, tragic journal.

"Let me go, please. I'm used to making it without money. Lots of it, anyway. I don't even know anything about my family because I don't have one."

Mr. Chandler shook his head. "Everyone has a family."

"Where's Tom?"

"Your boyfriend is no longer a concern of yours."

Except he wasn't her boyfriend. She'd never had a chance to explain about Peyton, not that it mattered. She didn't care if Tom wasn't a college graduate, didn't have "prospects" and such. As long as he worked hard, she'd take him like he was. Her throat hurt. *Lord, please let me get the chance to tell him. I love him.*

Aloud, she said, "He's not my boyfriend." Her voice held the tiniest quaver. "Don't hurt him."

"He'll be fine . . . if he wakes up in time, that is." Mr. Chandler set the flashlight on the bureau. "A pity the power's out, with the storm getting ready to break. Lucky me, just in the right time."

He struck a match and lit the lantern. "There. Here's a bit of light for you."

Her breath came in gasps, flickers of memory from Jenks. A thunderstorm. A dark closet. A locked door. Mom's screams. "Let me go, please."

"Say goodnight, Ms. Frost." He picked up the lantern, and let it gently roll onto its side on the wool carpet. With a whoosh, flames rose up from the antique fabric. "Au revoir." He turned on his heel and left.

Kelly screamed. All she could hear was the whoosh of flames devouring the curtains, the sound swallowing up William Chandler's footsteps descending the stairs. She heard a door close.

"Help me!" She didn't know if anyone could hear her. One of her legs felt as if the rope was loosening. She kept kicking. Okay. Her left foot came free of the rope. But how long before smoke would claim the rest of the oxygen in the room?

She worked at the rope tying her other ankle, jamming her left toes into her ankle. He'd tied the knots, but not too tight. Clever man. If he knew she could free herself in time, the smoke might get her, and then it would look as if she'd died crawling for safety.

She screamed again. As if anyone could hear her. Enough of that, using precious oxygen. Her other ankle was free now. She tried to sling her legs off the bed. If she could somehow pull the posters from the bed, maybe she'd have a chance. That was a big if.

The thick curtains went up like two pairs of torches. Maybe, just maybe, someone could see that from the street. Except she'd closed the front shutters that faced east, so the sun wouldn't bother her first thing in the morning.

The security system. Didn't it have a panic button to call the fire department? If she could make it down to the entryway . . .

Her breath came in wheezes. Where was Tom? What had Chandler done to him? Drugged his drink, like he'd drugged hers? She should have known, should have listened to that warning inside that told her the man was up to no good. But then, she was a suspicious person anyway . . .

She heard pounding and the sound of splintering wood. Her breath was worth one more scream. Oh, what would they tell Lottie? Tears burned her eyes as she inhaled a lungful of acrid air and tried to form a sound. It came out more like a moan than a scream.

Someone stumbled into the room.

"Help me," Kelly said. Her eyes burned.

It was Tom, and his hands were bleeding. "Kelly."

"He's crazy, gone crazy." She yanked at the ropes.

"Hang on." Tom worked at one of the knots and it came free. "He was . . . never a Boy Scout."

Kelly reached for her other wrist, but her hands refused to work. "Tom . . ."

"Hush. Save your breath. There's not much air left."

Panes of glass shattered, making both of them duck. Flames danced across the ceiling, devouring fresh oxygen from outside, reaching for her hair. Kelly grabbed Mary's journal from the top of the chest.

"The quilt," she managed to gasp. "We've got to get Mary's quilt."

They stumbled into the hallway. Flames raced up the front staircase to meet them.

"No good," Tom said. "The back stairs, from the servants' quarters to the kitchen."

At least the air was relatively clear. Kelly stumbled. Tom slid his arm around her waist, pulling her to his side. They skidded to a stop at the bottom of the stairs and collided with the wooden door, blocking them from the kitchen.

Tom pushed the door. "He's boarded it shut or something." He rammed it with his shoulder. The air grew thick, warm.

Kelly glanced over her shoulder. An orange glow lit the hallway above. "We're running out of time." A faint wail of a siren drifted down the stairwell.

"I hope not." Tom aimed, then kicked at the door again.

"Let me try, too." She joined him at the bottom step, the closed door flush with the step's edge. Sweat matted her hair to her forehead. She took some breaths of the smoke-filled air, as if she were sucking through a broken straw.

"Okay, on three." Tom angled his body so it faced her. "Give it . . . all you've got."

Kelly nodded.

"One, two, three."

They rammed into the door. Pain exploded through Kelly's shoulder. She gasped, stumbled on the bottom step. Her head cracked on something hard.

***

Tom landed on the vintage black-and-white kitchen tile. Kelly lay sprawled out beside him, her eyes closed. He touched her arm, and she moaned.

"Get the quilt . . . it's important. Please . . ." She coughed.

"We've got to leave it, get out of here." He tugged on her arm, and she screamed, grabbing her shoulder. "I'm sorry, I'm sorry. Here." He reached for her other side, hauled her to her feet.

"I can't leave it." She reached for Mary's journal on the floor. "It's in the ballroom."

Which was next to the dining room, one room away from the front of the house in flames. "I doubt they'll sue you for something that's not your fault."

"If you don't get it, I will." She leaned on him and he pulled her close.

"Stubborn woman." But he hauled her to the back door.

"No." She stumbled toward the ballroom, away from safety. "You don't understand. It's for your family, too. Our family."

He followed her to the ballroom, noticing his bloody hands for the first time. "I can't touch it."

The smell of smoke filled the hallway, and yellow flames met them halfway. Kelly darted into the ballroom, headed for the worktable. "You're coming with me." She unbound it from the rack.

The sound of splintering wood filled the air. "The front of the house is going to collapse. We need to move."

**193**

Kelly freed the quilt. "Got it," she gasped. She limped toward him. "I . . . I can't breathe."

His own breaths made his lungs burn. He coughed, sucking in more of the deadly air. "We're almost home free." He turned to see the way they'd come engulfed in flames. "We're not going that way." He tugged Kelly's hand and pulled her across the ballroom toward one of the large doors.

"How?" Kelly stopped, her weight sinking against him.

"Give me the quilt." He took it from her hands. "Wrap up."

"What?"

He wheezed as he pulled the quilt over her head. He had so much to say, when lately he couldn't think of anything other than her apparent betrayal. His words would keep for later. "Hold on tight."

Covered with the quilt, she almost looked like a ghost in his arms. He picked her up and ran for the nearest floor to ceiling ballroom window. Shattering glass, splintering wood, more pain. Kelly's scream.

Cool air, mercifully cooler, rushed into his lungs. Tom and Kelly landed on the patio that ran the length of the house. Shouts filled the air. The flashing strobe of fire trucks lit the night. Lightning flashed, thunder pulsed. The downpour started as if an unseen hand turned a faucet above them.

*Thank you, thank you, Lord.* Tom lay on his back, coughed, and reached for Kelly.

The quilt lay around her shoulders. She moved as if in a daze, sat up and pushed the quilt away. "Tom . . ."

"You folks stay right where you are," a voice said. "EMS is on the way. Is there anyone else in the house?" A firefighter approached, clad in his gear.

"No." Tom shook his head. "But this is arson, deliberately set. William Chandler did it. Find him." His voice rose, but then cut off when the cough started.

"Calm down, now." The man's focus shifted to Kelly. "Miss, are you all right?"

Kelly sank back onto the grass, half on the quilt, half off, wheezing and coughing. Tom leaned over her, brushing her hair away from her forehead. "Kelly?"

She gave a gasp, and sucked in a rattling breath. "I love you, Tom."

The sound of shattering glass made Tom look toward the house. When he looked back at Kelly, her breathing was still.

"No!" His shout sounded like a man in agony.

# 20

Her cough followed her all the way to Lottie's home in Haverhill. On Saturday morning, Kelly woke up in her old bedroom that had been occupied by at least four more foster children since she had lived there. Or maybe it wasn't Saturday. After time in the hospital, her days had run together, unmeasured.

Black gunk kept coming up with the worst of the coughing fits and whenever she blew her nose. She sat up when she saw the clock on the nightstand. Ten a.m. . . . She never let herself sleep that late. The quick movement triggered another coughing spasm. Kelly grabbed a tissue from the nightstand.

The door burst open and Lottie came in. "You're awake."

Kelly nodded. "The quilt? Where's the quilt?" She glanced around the room.

"It's here, right here. I found a box and got some acid-free tissue." Lottie shook her head. "It smells like smoke and it's a mess."

But it had helped save her life, helped both her and Tom fight their way through the smoke. She didn't care if Firstborn Holdings, LLC, came after her. They could have the quilt. They were the ones who'd assigned a whack-job to keep tabs on Gray House.

"I haven't decided what to do with it yet."

"Well, you have a visitor coming soon, someone you'll want to meet, I'm sure."

"Not a reporter or anything . . ." She recalled the flash of cameras and news trucks on County Street, filming Gray House as it burned. "Say, how did you get the quilt?" She'd lost track of it somewhere in the ambulance.

"Tom Pereira. What a wonderful young man," said Lottie. "He was frantic to know how you were, but I told him to give you some time."

"Thank you." The memory of their kiss in the rose garden, right before Peyton showed up to spoil everything, made her cheeks grow hot. What Tom must think of her. She remembered her gasped confession of her love, right after he'd helped rescue her from the house and right before she passed out. Of course, he'd rescued her. Guys like Tom Pereira were the good ones. And she'd told him she loved him, without any explanation about Peyton.

Like Mary Gray, she wrestled with absolution from what she had done in her moments of weakness. Unlike Mary Gray, she'd been deceived. Mary had walked into things with Esteban with her eyes wide open and carrying an empty heart. Ironic that her descendant, William Chandler, had also tried to burn away what he couldn't deal with anymore.

The idea of Gray House in ruins made her heart hurt. The place should be open for all to see and hear the story of Mary Gray, not locked up like a mausoleum.

"So," she found her voice at last. "Who's coming?"

"Your great-great-grandfather."

"My what?" The man would have to be at least one hundred years old. And she never knew anything about a great-great-grandfather. She supposed she had eight of them at one time but never imagined she would know one.

"Jonas Plummer is the owner of Firstborn Holdings," Lottie said with a sigh. She sank onto the small wooden chair where Kelly had sat and worked at her homework eons ago.

"I've met Jonas Plummer." Kelly's head began to pound. "The owner of Gray House is my great-great-grandfather? I don't understand."

"He was the one who checked up on you here and called when you first moved to New Bedford." Lottie frowned. "He sounds like he's not well, but he was determined to speak to you in person."

Kelly nodded as she studied Lottie's downcast expression. "Lottie, what's wrong?"

"It's silly." The older woman shook her head.

"What is it? Is it about Mr. Plummer?"

"He's your blood family. I know how you've been aching inside for a family, a real family." Lottie's eyes filled with tears. "But sweetie, Chuck and I, we always wanted you for our family."

"But . . . but you never adopted me."

"You were already almost grown. We always had a special place for you in our hearts, never having a daughter of our own." A tear rolled down Lottie's cheek. "We were never supposed to prefer one of our kids over the other, but you were always our favorite. Our girl. Our Kelly."

"I . . . I didn't know." But of course she'd known, deep down, and she'd pushed it away.

"Then you were done with high school and so determined to make it on your own, without anyone's help." Lottie shrugged. "What could we do but let you go? And now, here comes Mr. Plummer."

Now Kelly wiped a tear away. "Lottie, I'm sorry." She rose from the bed and winced, remembering her sprained ankle. "I didn't mean to push you away like I did. I don't know why I did. I always felt like I was on the outside looking in."

"You were never outside with us," Lottie whispered.

Kelly hugged her. "Thanks . . . Momma." The word shot into a tender place in her heart and she sobbed. "I'm so sorry. I wish Chuck were still alive to know."

"It's okay. He always told me you'd realize it one day. He knew." Lottie nodded after they ended the hug. "Well, Mr. Plummer should be here soon. I'd get myself ready if I were you."

A million questions rattled in Kelly's brain. How long had this man known about her? Why didn't he come for her, rescue her out of the horror she'd lived in with her mother and a countless string of boyfriends? *God, please, help me stay calm.* But her hands shook as she picked up a fresh bath towel on her way to the shower.

---

Tom tightened his grip on the steering wheel. Driving through Boston had been enough to make a man break out in hives. Forget the seizures. This was enough to drive a man crazy.

"We're almost there, Mr. Plummer."

The elderly man in the passenger seat nodded slowly. "No rush. This has been a lifetime in the making."

"A lifetime, huh?"

"It's time to right some wrongs." He sucked down some oxygen from the portable tank beside him. "The doctor would have a fit if he knew I was traveling like this."

"You told me you could travel." Tom found it easy not to be irritated by the man. But still, what if something were to happen to him?

"Of course I can." Mr. Plummer shifted on the seat. "I can do whatever I want. I'm half-dead already."

"That's not a nice way to joke, sir." Tom shook his head, and the GPS chimed for him to turn. "Why didn't you just summon us to meet you instead of having your wacko nephew do it?"

"Protocol, Son, protocol. Or should I call you my cousin, how many times removed?" Mr. Plummer cleared his throat. "Don't you young people know anything about protocol? I needed to see if you were genuine. Many people would like to be a part of this, and I can't let it go to just anyone. Not even my nephew."

Tom gritted his teeth. Chandler had been caught, and they'd found evidence enough to hold him in jail, without bail. Arson, two counts of attempted murder. And that was just the short list. Tom shoved his anger aside. He'd missed Kelly so bad it was a physical ailment. What they'd been through together, and how he'd treated her after that scumbag Peyton had shown up. He should have known better than to fall for the guy's song and dance about how he and Kelly should get back together.

He had a lot to apologize for. But his turn would come after the elderly man beside him had his chance.

"You going to stay on, Son?" asked the old man.

"Stay on?"

"Groundskeeper of Gray House."

"Uh, if you didn't notice, Gray House is literally half the place it used to be." Sad it was, really, to see the gaping hole in the front portion of the house where the bulk of the fire had raged. Between the fire department and a downpour, the flames had gone, leaving scars behind.

"You're going to rebuild though, correct?"

"Me? I'm not a builder." Tom followed the GPS. Another half mile, according to the screen. Zigzagging through the Haverhill streets, they'd be there soon enough.

"But you can supervise." The old man coughed again, this time spasms of coughing interrupting his speech. "The lawn is in rough shape, too, after all those firefighters dragged hoses and stomped all over it."

"Huh. Well, I'll have to think about it." He just wanted to hop on his bike and go. Somewhere, anywhere. But here he was, driving up to a modest two-story home on a narrow street. Not upscale, and not the hood, either.

"Here we go, then," said the old man.

Tom killed the engine, then got out and helped the old man from the vehicle. He crept slowly, slowly, up the front walk, then carefully scaled the steps one by one. He stopped once, hanging on to the stair railing and swaying like a drunken sailor. Tom was about to reach out and help him along, but kept his hand at his side.

He let the old man reach the front door first and ring the bell. D-day for all of them, in more than one way. He'd been hard on Kelly, and now he was facing her for the first time since the fire. He had no idea what to say.

The inner door opened, and Kelly stood there looking fresh and clean, her hair smooth and shining as it draped past her shoulders.

"Come in." Her voice sounded tight as she opened the storm door. "Lottie's made some sandwiches, three kinds. Plus her homemade lemonade, which is the best. She's on the back porch, setting things up."

She watched them enter, the old man shuffling and Tom contemplating whether or not to bolt and hop back in the car. Only it wasn't his car, and he wasn't about to get arrested for car theft.

He followed them through the house that smelled like pie, with a whiff of lemon cleaner. "This is where you grew up?"

"Uh, sort of," Kelly said as she faced him. "I lived here during junior high and high school. Never knew how good I had it, either." She shrugged and gave him a half grin.

The old man shuffled to a stop. "I think you two young people need to have a chat. I'll find my way to Miss Lottie and some lemonade."

"But, sir—," Tom began.

"No buts. I might be an invalid, but I'm not dead just yet." The old man waved at him and continued along the hallway.

Kelly folded her arms across her chest. "So, he is my great-great-grandfather, right?"

"Your great-great-grandfather?" Tom gazed after the man.

She nodded. "Through my mother's side of the family. We verified it for sure. It turns out there's more to the story. He's, uh . . . he's directly related to Captain Hiram Gray."

"Whaa?" Tom shook his head.

"I was looking for Mary Gray's baby, the one she gave away to her lover's family to raise."

"My great-great-great grandfather?" Tom shook his head. "Whoa. This is a lot to process. So we're related, distantly, via Mary Gray way, way back there."

"I'm a closer relative. Little Hiram Junior was my great-great-grandfather. Hiram grew up and fathered a daughter, who married a Plummer. Only children, girls, straight down the family line to me. Except for Chandler's mother." She let her arms relax. "So when Chandler was checking up on his great-uncle's choices of employees—you and me—he freaked out when he realized we're both connected to Gray House. Then Plummer decided to change his will and include us. Or so I've heard."

Tom allowed himself to reach for her hand. "Kelly."

She stared at his hand. "Tom, I didn't know Peyton was married. He kept it from me. I'd . . . I'd never had a real boyfriend before. I'd been too shy, too scared. I think toward the end with Peyton, I was in denial, and then I was so ashamed, and then Jonna found out, and I should have told you—"

He pulled her close and silenced her with a kiss. He let himself run his fingers through the silken strands of her hair, not cutting short the kiss like last time in the garden. Her arm crept around his neck.

"I'm sorry," he said. "I'm sorry I didn't want to listen."

"Apology accepted." Then she coughed.

"Are you okay?" he asked, still holding her in his arms.

"Much better now." Then she kissed him back.

# Epilogue

*One year later*

Gray House was nearly complete. Long months of construction, even through the wintertime, but Tom insisted they stay on track. The old man would have wanted it that way. The old man, even from the grave his body occupied since last fall, a mere two months after the fire, was still getting his way.

Gray House would open for overnight guests and tours, with Mary Gray's quilt kept in a place of honor, framed in the front hallway. Kelly had painstakingly tried to repair it again. The results told them it would never function as a quilt again, its last comforting act protecting Kelly while Tom pulled them both through the window glass during the fire. Maybe that was the way it was meant to be.

God help him, he never wanted to let the regrets pile up over the years like the old man had. He'd spent so much time shutting out the family he did have, just like the old man. He was grateful to God every day that he'd wised up.

Otherwise he'd have never opened his heart to Kelly. Here she came, the back of her car filled with bags and such. Turn her loose in a home improvement store, and the shopping beast came out.

She bounced from the car and into his arms. "Mr. Pereira, wait until you see what I found for the dining room."

"What's that, Mrs. Pereira?"

"A table, just like the one ruined in the fire. Happy six months' anniversary." She grinned at him and planted a saucy kiss on his lips. If she kept at him like that, he'd never get the wood trim on the porch done but they'd end up back at their apartment, enjoying newlywed life.

"Is it in the car?"

"No, goofy, they're going to deliver it later." Kelly faced the house. "I can't believe we're going to move in, that Gray House is ours."

"Yours."

"*Ours.*"

"I wish the old man could see it now."

"Maybe he can, somehow." Kelly reached for Tom's hand and placed it on her stomach. "I was thinking, if our baby is a boy, we could name him Jonas?"

"Baby?"

"Uh-huh." Kelly grinned that megawatt smile at him. "He, or she, can grow up in Gray House."

Tom swept her into his arms. A baby. A son, a daughter, it didn't matter.

The old was gone, the new had come.

Tom had quit questioning these many months, had let the old dreams die and released them to the depths of his memory. The future, though, lay bright as the morning sun shining up over the harbor, its course held securely in the sights of their heavenly father.

# Discussion Questions

1. Kelly has an industry rival who caused trouble and still carries a grudge. Have you ever had a coworker or colleague who always seemed to be competing against you? How did you handle that?

2. Because of his past failures, Tom tended to isolate himself from his loving family. What are some ways you can appreciate your family and interact with them, flaws and all?

3. At the beginning of the book, Kelly is broke and has car trouble. She hopes this new job will be an answer to those troubles and reignite her sputtering career. If you've had tough financial times, what has given you hope that eventually things will turn around?

4. Tom faces obstacles—emotionally and sometimes physically—and he's afraid to try something new, like going to college. What kind of advice would you give to help him set a goal and strive for it?

5. Kelly believes the quilt is mostly unsalvageable, but she pushes through and works on restoring it as much as possible. What are some ways you've completed what might have seemed like an impossible project?

6. Both Kelly and Tom don't know much about their family genealogies. What kinds of stories have you uncovered about your ancestors?

7. Sometimes family doesn't mean being related by blood. Kelly discovers the family of her heart has been supporting and loving her all along. Who has been that kind of family in your life?

8. Jonas Plummer has many regrets, and he knows his days on earth are drawing to a close. He thinks leaving a financial legacy to his family will make up for his

coldness in earlier years. What would you tell someone like Jonas, to encourage him?

9. Mary Gray made some disastrous choices that affected not just her immediate family but the generations that followed. How can God redeem the consequences of bad choices for those who are affected by them?

10. Kelly is haunted for a long time by her own bad decisions and the consequences that followed. What Scriptures can help someone who has a hard time forgiving themselves?

Want to learn more about author
Lynette Sowell and check out other great
fiction from Abingdon Press?

Sign up for our fiction newsletter at
www.AbingdonPress.com
to read interviews with your favorite authors, find tips
for starting a reading group, and stay posted on what
new titles are on the horizon. It's a place to connect
with other fiction readers or post a
comment about this book.

Be sure to visit Lynette online!

Facebook: www.facebook.com/lynettesowellauthor
Twitter: @LynetteSowell   https://twitter.com/LynetteSowell
Pinterest: LynetteSowell
www.pinterest.com/quiltsoflove/tempest-s-course-by-
lynette-sowell/

And now for a sneak peek at

## *Scraps of Evidence*

### by Barbara Cameron

## From the new Quilts of Love Series.

—∞—

# 1

Tess fought back a yawn as she walked into her aunt's hospital room. Excitement had kept her awake half the night.

"I told you not to come," her aunt said when she saw Tess. But she smiled.

"I wanted to." She bent down and kissed her cheek. "You're my favorite aunt."

"I'm your only aunt."

"Still my favorite."

Tess pulled a chair up to the side of the bed and set the tote bag she carried on the floor. "What did the doctor say?"

"No concussion. But I have to stay another day for observation. Doctors," she muttered, her mouth turning down at the corners.

Tess studied her aunt's pale face. Sometimes when she looked at Katherine she missed her mother so much it hurt. She didn't know what she'd do if she lost her, too.

She shook off the thought. Her aunt was just in her late fifties and in good health. There was no reason to believe she wouldn't be around for a long time.

"Big day today, huh?"

"The biggest. It's what I've been working toward since I graduated from the police academy."

Her aunt reached for her hand and squeezed it. "I'm happy for you."

"Brought you something."

"You shouldn't have. You look tired."

"Gee. Thanks." She pulled the makeup bag from the tote and her aunt pounced on it.

"Oh, thank goodness!" Katherine cried. "They gave me a comb, but a girl needs her lipstick to feel human."

She pulled out a compact, opened it, and grimaced. "Oh my, it's worse than I thought."

Using her forefinger, she dabbed some concealer cream on the delicate skin under one eye, then shook her head.

"Going to have a bit of a shiner there," she said with a sigh. She patted on some powder, applied some lipstick, then smiled at her appearance. "Not bad."

"You look great. No one expects you to look like a beauty queen in the hospital."

"One must keep up one's appearance," Katherine said, folding her hands primly on top of the blanket covering her.

Aunt Katherine had always reminded Tess of Grace Kelly, the icy blond actress in the old movies they'd watched together years ago.

Tess was the opposite. She wore her blonde hair in a no-nonsense short cut, hated makeup, and instead of being dainty, had been five-foot-ten since high school. Oh, and there was that ten unwanted pounds that persisted in sticking around no matter what she did.

Her aunt turned the mirror on Tess. "Forgot something?"

She wanted to roll her eyes, but decided not to. With a big sigh, Tess pulled a tube of lip gloss out of her pocket and swiped it across her mouth.

"My, my, don't be primping so much," her aunt said with a touch of sarcasm as Tess tucked the tube back in her pocket.

"Makeup just slides right off my face in this heat."

"I like your new look."

Tess stared down at her lightweight navy jacket and slacks worn with a crisp white shirt. She liked what it represented more. Not that she'd ever minded wearing a uniform. It was what had gotten her to this point. Now she simply wore a different one.

She reached down and withdrew a blue quilt from the tote bag and placed it on her aunt's lap. "I thought you might like to have it here to remind you of home."

Her aunt brightened, and she tried to sit up. Tess sprang out of her chair, helped raise the bed a bit, and adjusted the pillow behind her aunt's head.

"Better?"

"Yes, thanks."

Tess watched as Katherine unfolded the quilt and stroked it. "It's my favorite."

"I know."

She raised a corner of it to her cheek and her eyes closed, then opened. "I'll never forget the day Gordon walked into my shop."

"He was this big, burly police officer," Tess prompted with a smile.

"So you've heard the story, eh?"

Tess laughed. "About a million times," she said.

Katherine nodded, but she smiled and didn't take offense.

"But tell it to me again." She leaned back in her chair.

"I thought he was coming to tell me I was illegally parked out front or something," her aunt said, her eyes beginning to take on a faraway look. "It was so hard to find parking because they were working on the street for the longest time. But he had this bag of scraps in his hands. Fabric scraps."

"Pieces from dresses worn by his sisters and mother."

"Um hmm. He thought his mother would enjoy having a quilt made of them. Mother's Day was coming up."

"So he brought in a few pieces each week, and you made the quilt."

"That's right." She examined the stitching on one square and then, apparently finding it satisfactory, tucked it around her. "Something just clicked into place. We had coffee a couple of times, began dating. We were married by the time Mother's Day rolled around."

"So Gordon's mother got two presents."

Katherine frowned. "I don't think she saw it that way. We weren't very good friends at first. Gordon could have been a little more diplomatic about letting her know our plans to get married."

Tess felt his presence before she saw him. She wasn't sure why but it had always been so.

"What's this, I'm not diplomatic?" Gordon said in his booming voice. He strolled into the room, a tall, big-boned man whose white dress shirt stretched tightly over his barrel chest.

Her aunt jumped. "Gordon! You startled me."

He just laughed, removed the toothpick dangling from his mouth, and bent to kiss her head. "Oh, stop the fussin', Kathy," he drawled.

"If you hadn't done that—" She stopped, pressed her lips tight and plucked at the quilt.

Gordon turned to Tess. "So, hear your new partner's due in today. Big-city guy, eh?"

"That's what I hear."

She watched him as he prowled around the room, peering at the bouquets her aunt had been sent. When he passed a mirror hung on one wall, he peered into it critically and checked his crew cut. The short strands stood at attention on his head as if not daring to lie down on the job.

Then he began moving around the room again, as if restless. He pulled a card from an arrangement of daisies and frowned at it. "Who's this Lee?"

"A woman at church."

"You sure?"

Katherine sighed. "Yes. You met her once. Lee Weatherby."

"Hmm. Yeah. I remember. Old biddy." He tucked the card back in the bouquet and glanced at his watch. "Gotta go. I'll check in on you later."

"You can't stay for a few minutes?"

He shook his head. "Have to see the chief. I'll check in on you later." He patted her head and turned to Tess. "You working tonight?"

"You know I am," she said mildly.

He grinned, removed his toothpick and tossed it in the trash. It missed, but he didn't slow down to pick it up on his way out of the room.

Tess turned to her aunt and saw that the woman watched her husband's exit with a mixture of sadness and bewilderment.

"Aunt Katherine?" She waited until she turned to look at her. She hesitated, then plunged ahead. "Is everything okay with you and Gordon?"

She raised her eyebrows. "Of course. Why do you ask such a question?"

"I still don't know how you got hurt."

"Oh, it was so silly," Katherine said. "I just tripped over Prissy, that's all. She always seems to be underfoot."

Prissy was a very spoiled Persian her aunt had had for many years. Tess had never known her to hang out anywhere but the sofa and around the food bowl. "You're sure?" Tess asked quietly.

"Of course." She looked over the side of the bed. "Now, I don't suppose you have anything else in that tote bag, do you?"

Laughing, Tess picked it up and handed it to her. Katherine grinned as she pulled out the quilt she was currently working on. Tess helped her spread it out, find her needles and thread in the sewing basket she'd brought. Then she sat back as her aunt happily began working.

"You didn't bring yours?"

Tess shook her head. "I knew I wouldn't have enough time. But maybe tomorrow. I'm off." She glanced at her watch. "I'm sorry, but I need to get going. Anything you need before I leave?"

"Not a thing. Oh, did you feed Prissy when you went by the house? Gordon forgets when I'm not home."

"Sure did." And Prissy had simply looked at her disdainfully from her place on the sofa.

Katherine held out her hands, and Tess took them. "Father, walk with Tess and protect her and keep her safe. Help her to do her job to the best of her ability. Thank you. Amen."

Tess squeezed her hands and smiled, then stood and hugged her. "See you tomorrow. Call me before then if you need anything."

The heat hit her like a wet blanket the minute she left the building. Another July in St. Augustine, oldest city in the country. She was that rare thing—a native Floridian—and in all her twenty-six years she couldn't remember a hotter one.

As much as she wanted to hurry into the air-conditioned haven of her car, she forced herself not to rush. Hurrying just made it feel hotter, and besides, she'd likely be out in the heat for much of the rest of the day. She started the car, turned the A/C on high, and knew she'd probably be at the station before the car cooled off.

A sightseeing tram pulled in front of her at the light beside the police station. The driver recognized Tess and she waved.

Tess smiled and muttered, "Hurry up," beneath her breath. Nothing was slower than the tram. Except for the horse-drawn carriages. Thankfully, none of those were in sight.

With time to spare, she pulled into the parking lot, gathered her things, and hurried inside.

Marlene from Records sat eating a sandwich in the break room. Tess stowed her lunch in the refrigerator.

"First day on the new job, huh? How's it feel?"

"Pretty good."

"Met the new guy yet?"

"Not yet."

Marlene fanned herself with her hand. "Hot."

Tess shook her head and left the room.

Two men stood just inside the roll call room, their backs turned to her.

"Ever had a female partner before?" she heard one of them ask.

She recognized the voice as belonging to Tom Smithers.

"No."

Tess froze, wondering what Smithers was going to say next.

"Well, you've got your work cut out for you, buddy," Smithers said, and he laughed.

The other man turned and he saw Tess. Her training had taught her to capture an impression quickly, and what she got was intense: his eyes were green and honed in on her, his posture military straight, and his stance at attention. He was tall, probably six-two, and like Marlene had said, he was hot: model pretty with black hair and an easy grin.

"Aw, heck, she's right behind me, isn't she?" Smithers asked when the man grinned.

He laughed. "What do you think?"

Stepping forward, he offered his hand. "Detective Villanova. Nice to meet you. I'm Logan McMillan."

---

She had a nice, firm grip and looked him straight in the eye. "Tess."

He liked the way she observed Smithers slinking off, muttering about getting some water. Maybe she was good at hiding her expression—well, actually, she better be because no cop survived without being good at keeping a non-emotional front—but she didn't waste a second on a glare at him or any kind of comment.

"Never a good idea to talk about someone," he said quietly as she looked down at the hand he still held.

She shrugged, but couldn't hold back a small smile. "And if you're going to do it, be bright enough not to stand with your back to the door."

Other officers began crowding in the door. Logan gestured for Tess to precede him in finding a seat and sat next to her. The shift supervisor went over the previous night's activity and bulletins, then introduced Logan.

He tried not to fidget as the supervisor read off his list of accomplishments. They sounded great, but in the end, did that sort of thing matter?

"So make him feel welcome to our fair city," the supervisor was saying. "Let's go out there and protect and serve, people. And stay safe."

"They say the same thing everywhere?" he whispered to Tess.

He rose when fellow officers stopped to introduce themselves on the way out of the room. Maybe it was a stereotype, but he had expected the officers in a tourist city would look more laid back.

The shift supervisor walked over. "Take a few hours to show Logan around, give him a feel for the city."

"Yes, sir."

They walked out and Tess stopped at the car. "Want to flip for who drives?"

"Why? I have no problem with you driving. Partner."

Her head snapped up and she gave him a measuring look. He smiled at her and got into the car. The second look came as no surprise after the comment by Smithers. Law enforcement was still a man's world in many communities.

"We're right in the historic district here," she said as she guided the car onto King Street. "It's not a big area, and during tourist season it's crowded. You have to keep your eyes peeled or it's easy to run over a jaywalker."

She gave him the standard tour. He debated telling her he'd taken it when he visited for the interview and decided not to at this point. Seeing the city through her eyes would give him a better perspective of it—and her.

"Years ago there was quite a debate over whether a new, modern-looking bridge should replace this one. Every so often somebody would get fed up with the traffic jams on the bridge," she said as they waited at the traffic light to drive over the bridge connecting downtown St. Augustine to Anastasia Island.

"The old bridge had deteriorated," she continued. "Finally, we got a new bridge, but it looks like the old one. The two Medici lions there were at the foot of the old bridge and now they guard this one."

She turned to him and smiled. "What other city has something like this?"

The light changed and just as they were halfway across, lights flashed and a gate came down, blocking traffic. The draw bridge went up as a boat passed beneath.

"You learn to pray that we don't have an emergency and get stuck on the bridge," she said as she drummed her fingers on the steering wheel.

The drive was short since the island was small. "If you're into lighthouses you'll have to climb this one," she said, waving at the tall structure whose base was painted with a winding black-on-white design. "The view up there is something else."

She made a U-turn and glanced at him briefly. "We locals don't go doing stuff like that in the middle of summer."

She drove across the bridge and turned right to take them past Castillo de San Marcos, the old fort, a huge structure built of coquina stone that had stood guard over the city for hundreds of years. Horse-drawn carriages were parked along the right side of the road, and she watched carefully in case one of them was about to pull out onto the road.

"This city has a history of violence," she said as she parked so that he could look up at the fort. "Matanzas Bay. Matanzas means blood. At the same time, we have more churches per capita than any other city in the country."

A horse-drawn carriage passed on the road and the driver waved at Tess. "That was my first job when I attended Flagler College," she told him. "I loved it."

"So that's where you learned to be a tour guide."

She gave him a brief smile. "Can't help but be one when you grow up here. I should warn you: every relative you have will want to come visit you now that you live in Florida."

"No one to visit. Mother died two years ago, and I was an only child."

"Father?"

"Serving overseas somewhere."

He sensed she was curious, but she didn't press him. "You?"

"My mother died several years ago, and I never knew my dad. My only relative is my aunt. Her husband is Gordon Baxter. Have you met him yet?"

"He sat in on the interview with the chief." Logan hadn't been impressed with her uncle and was a little relieved the man wasn't a blood relation of Tess's.

She nodded. "He and the chief are tight."

They drove around for another hour, and she filled him in on crime statistics and insider information about the city.

"Dinner break?"

"Sounds good. You choose."

"Seafood?"

"Seafood sounds good."

"Place not too far from here has the best shrimp in the county."

"Sounds good."

"Just ignore all the tourist schtick. You know, the mermaid paintings. Nautical décor."

A few minutes later, they were settled in a booth with tall glasses of sweet tea and smoked mullet dip before them.

Logan ignored the menu and let Tess's order of a dozen shrimp—fried—and sides of cole slaw and French fries guide him.

"And hushpuppies?" the waitress asked him.

Tess groaned.

"Problem?" Logan asked.

"No," said Tess.

Pam laughed. "I'll just bring you one. One can't hurt."

"I can't ever stop at one."

The waitress looked at Logan. "Guard your plate. Girl steals them right off it when you're not looking. Seen it too many times. Outright larceny." Chuckling, she left them to put in the order.

Logan took a sip of his tea. "So, Tess. Why'd you get into law enforcement?"

Her fingers tightened on her glass and she frowned. She set the glass down on the table. "My best friend was murdered my senior year in high school."

She traced the condensation on the side of her glass and frowned. "The killer's never been found."

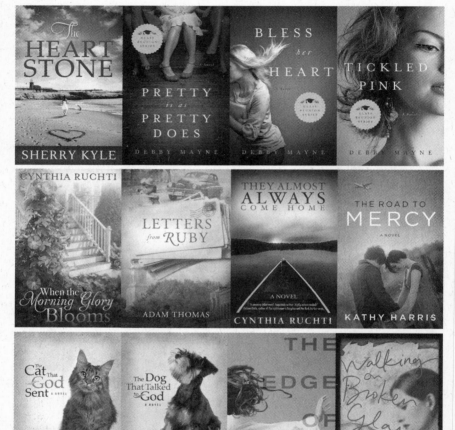